this can't be happening!

MACDONALD HALL

The Macdonald Hall Series

GORDON KORMAN

this can't be happening!

MACDONALD HALL

Previous title:
This Can't Be Happening at Macdonald Hall!

Cover photos by
Rodrigo Moreno and Luis Borba

Photo-illustration by
Yüksel Hassan

Scholastic Canada Ltd.
Toronto New York London Auckland Sydney
Mexico City New Delhi Hong Kong Buenos Aires

Scholastic Canada Ltd.
175 Hillmount Road, Markham, Ontario L6C 1Z7, Canada

Scholastic Inc.
555 Broadway, New York, NY 10012, USA

Scholastic Australia Pty Limited
PO Box 579, Gosford, NSW 2250, Australia

Scholastic New Zealand Limited
Private Bag 94407, Greenmount, Auckland, New Zealand

Scholastic Ltd.
Villiers House, Clarendon Avenue, Leamington Spa,
Warwickshire CV32 5PR, UK

National Library of Canada Cataloguing in Publication

Korman, Gordon
This can't be happening! / Gordon Korman.
ISBN 0-439-97429-1
I. Title.
PS8571.O78T5 2003   jC813'.54   C2002-904965-2 PZ7

6 5 4 3 2 1   Printed in Canada   03 04 05 06 07

For Mr. Hamilton

contents

Chapter 1

"it's always us!"

East of Toronto, just off Highway 48, you will find a beautiful tree-lined campus right across the road from the famous Miss Scrimmage's Finishing School for Young Ladies. It is Macdonald Hall, where generations of boys have been educated and prepared for manhood. Named for Sir John A. Macdonald, the Hall, with its ivy-covered stone buildings and beautiful rolling lawns, is the most respected boarding school for boys in all of Canada.

In Canada? you say. Why, then, is the flagpole in front of the Faculty Building proudly flying the flag of Malbonia?

The answer lies in Dormitory 3, room 306.

* * *

The window blinds were drawn, but that did not prevent two sets of attentive eyes from peering through the small cracks. They were fixed on the area in front of the Faculty Building.

"Nobody's even noticed it yet. You'd think this was Malbonia," grumbled Bruno Walton.

"Let's give it a little time," came the soothing voice of his roommate, Boots O'Neal.

Just then the Headmaster's blue Ford turned into the driveway. Instead of driving on into the parking lot, it screeched to a halt in front of the flagpole. The window rolled down and a familiar head emerged.

"This is it!" Bruno exclaimed.

The two boys watched as Mr. Sturgeon got out of his car and stared at the flag as if hoping it would vanish if he looked at it long enough.

"He sure doesn't look very happy," Boots observed.

"The Fish never looks happy," countered Bruno.

"No, not unless he's expelling somebody," Boots agreed. Among the boys at Macdonald Hall Mr. Sturgeon was notorious for his sternness, although to their parents he seemed a kind and understanding administrator who was fond of his students — he just never let them know it.

The two boys strained for a better view. A crowd was beginning to gather around the Headmaster, who was still staring at the flag as though willing it to be the red Maple Leaf of Canada.

Bruno jumped up from his spot at the window.

"Okay, everything's in motion. Let's go out and join the crowd."

"Not me," said Boots, beginning to perspire. "The Fish will know it's us."

"Don't be silly! How on earth could he know?"

"It's always us!" Boots exclaimed.

"Come on," Bruno said, pulling his friend up and half-dragging him down the freshly painted hallway. "We did all the work and they're having all the fun. Maybe it'll turn into a riot. I love riots."

The boys emerged into the yard and melted into the crowd. They could see the entire population of Miss Scrimmage's Finishing School watching from across the road. There was a lot of whistling, shouting and waving from the boys, until Mr. Sturgeon began surveying the students with his steely grey eyes. A hush fell. Boots pinched Bruno; the steely eyes had stopped on them.

At that moment the flag of Malbonia was unceremoniously lowered and the Maple Leaf run up in its place — but not before a number of spectators arriving for the big game had noticed it.

*　*　*

The annual hockey game between the Macdonald Hall Macs and the York Academy Cougars was to take place that afternoon. It had been a tradition since 1952, and the feeling of rivalry was intense. Spectators from both sides were pouring in, not just the families of the teams, but everyone who wanted to witness the yearly battle. The Macs were determined to win this one — having been thoroughly trounced in each of their five previous meetings. Then there was that wretched cat! The Cougars had a mascot, a thirty-pound alley cat sporting the team colours. At every game she would sit smugly on the players' bench looking fat and contented. It was too much! Macdonald Hall had no mascot at all — except for a loud cheering section from Miss Scrimmage's.

Two of the Macs' best players, Bruno Walton and Captain Boots O'Neal, were not yet in the dressing room. They were sneaking down the hall of Dormitory 3, trying to subdue a strangely active laundry bag. They stumbled into their room and locked the door behind them.

"All right, let 'er loose," gasped Bruno.

"Let her loose?" Boots screeched. "She'll rip the room up!"

"No, she won't. I'll give her a saucer of milk."

"A bucket would be more like it! All right, here goes!"

The cat erupted from the bag, swiping at Boots' face and scratching him from ear to chin.

"Yeow! Stupid cat!" Boots howled, backing away. The animal stretched, then leapt up onto the bed where it began making strange groaning noises.

"Do you think we hurt her?" Boots asked, rubbing his face.

"Nah, she's probably just overfed. I'm sure they stuff her before games so she can look extra fat on their bench."

"She'd better be all right," said Boots doubtfully.

"She's fine. C'mon, let's get going. We're late!"

As they entered the dressing room, Bruno and Boots gave their teammates the high sign — the first phase of 'Operation Fat Cat' had been successfully completed.

"You two are late!" Coach Flynn roared. "What's that scratch on your face, O'Neal?"

"I cut myself shaving," Boots mumbled, leaning over to tighten his shin pads.

Before the coach could respond, the dressing room was filled with laughter. Then the team was called out onto the ice.

Bruno and Boots skated their warm-up close together. From the corner of his mouth Boots hissed, "That scratch on my face is like wearing a sign saying I took the cat."

"Relax," Bruno said. "I won't let you take all the blame."

"Thanks, that's *very* comforting!"

Suddenly the loudspeaker burst into life: *Attention, please. We regret to announce the disappearance of the York Academy mascot. She is a large grey tabby wearing an orange and black ribbon and a tag bearing the name Myrtle. We would remind the gentlemen of Macdonald Hall that the York Academy team are our guests. We ask that Myrtle be returned immediately to the Cougars' bench.*

"We're in for it now!" groaned Boots. "The Fish is looking straight at us!"

"Just wait until they play the anthem," Bruno replied. Boots' heart sank; he had forgotten about that. The loudspeaker broke in again: *Would everyone please rise for our national anthem.* There was the usual scuffling of feet and buzzing of speakers. Then a hush fell over the arena. But instead of the solemn opening bars of *O Canada* the air exploded with the throbbing beat of *The Strip.* Miss Scrimmage's cheering section went wild. The girls started to bump and grind while their Headmistress swooned back into her seat. Even when the recording was finally switched off the hubbub continued.

Boots could almost feel Mr. Sturgeon's glare burning into his back. He did the only thing he could think of: standing at attention, he started to sing *O Canada.* Bruno got the message and quickly joined in; soon both teams were singing. The spectators followed suit and order was finally restored.

The game began in typical fashion: Boots got a goal and Bruno got a penalty. The Cougars struck back to even the score. It was still 1–1 when the first period ended.

In the dressing room Coach Flynn started into his pep talk. "We've got them, boys!" he bawled. "They're playing like a bunch of rejects today!"

Bruno raised innocent eyes to the coach. "That's because they don't have that stupid elephant cat." Flynn glared at the players. "I hope none of you had anything to do with that cat's disappearance."

"No, sir!" said Pete Anderson, the goalie. "We have better things to do than play with kittens." As Coach Flynn continued his harangue, Pete nudged Boots and his voice sank to a whisper. "What'd you do with it?"

"It's in our room," Boots muttered. "The last I saw of it, it looked as if it was dying!"

"Better not! What would we do with a hot dead cat?" Before Boots could reply, the buzzer sounded and the teams took the ice for the second period. Boots and the Cougars' captain met at centre ice for the face-off. The Cougar boy stared at Boots' face, then suddenly dropped his stick and gloves and wrestled Boots to the ice.

"Where'd you get that scratch?" he screamed. "Where's Myrtle?"

When the referee finally stopped the fight, the Cougars' captain was thrown out of the game for unsportsmanlike conduct. But from then on all the Cougars were after Boots. Only his speed and Bruno's weight saved him. At the end of the second period, the Macs were ahead by two goals.

In the dressing room Coach Flynn gave the team another rousing pep talk. At the end of it he turned to Boots and said, "As for you, O'Neal, I know darn well you're too young to be shaving. So if that scratch comes from a cat, I don't want to know about it." Boots remained silent.

As the teams poured onto the ice for the third period, Boots skated over to Bruno. "Do you think the coach will mention this to The Fish?"

"Who cares?" Bruno crowed. "We're going to win for the first time in six years!"

Boots was about to protest when the buzzer sounded. No sooner was play under way than he took a viciously hard cross-check from a revenge-seeking Cougar. Seconds later an egg came sailing out of the crowd and splattered all over the Cougar's sweater. It wasn't hard to locate the source of the egg: Miss Scrimmage looked as if she wanted to crawl into a hole. Cries of "Attaboy, girls!" and "That's showing 'em!" erupted from the Macs' bench. The offender headed for the penalty box with yolk dripping down onto his skates.

When the final buzzer ended the game, the arena rang with cheers. The Macs had won, 4–1. As Mr. Sturgeon pushed through the crowd, his expression alternated between a victory smirk and a grim mask.

Bruno and Boots showered and dressed hurriedly, mumbling something about having to study. It was time to plant Myrtle on the Cougars' bus. They raced to their room, let themselves in, and stopped dead. There, still on

Boots' bed, was Myrtle — with five kittens!

"Look!" Bruno gasped. "We're a father!"

"And I thought she was sick! I wish she had been! How are we going to get all of them back on the bus?"

"Same way," Bruno decided. "In the laundry bag."

Recalling Boots' scratch, he put on his hockey gloves and began to pack mother and kittens into the bag. Then the two boys stole out of the building and over to the Cougars' bus.

"I'll unload them. You stand guard," Bruno ordered.

A few seconds later, while Bruno was arranging the cats comfortably under a seat, he heard an ominously loud voice say, "Good evening, Mr. Sturgeon. Did you enjoy the game, sir?"

"Very much indeed," the Headmaster replied cordially. "And may I ask what you are doing at the Cougars' bus?"

Before Boots could reply, Bruno emerged. "I knew it, sir! I just knew it! Those York guys didn't even look for their precious mascot. The nerve of them, accusing us of kidnapping! Look, there she is, right over there. She just hid under a seat to have her kittens."

Mr. Sturgeon smiled crookedly. "Well, I'm extremely relieved to learn that none of the Macdonald boys stooped so low as to kidnap a mascot."

"We don't need *that* kind of help to beat them," Bruno replied.

"Just the same, I think you two had better run along," said Mr. Sturgeon. "I wouldn't want to see you accused of any hanky-panky just because you happen to be on the scene." Again his face adjusted itself into a very strange smile.

"Yes, sir!" the two chorused, and ran off to their room.

"Boy!" exclaimed Boots. "Were we lucky to get through this day alive!"

Bruno was rolling on his bed, hysterical with laughter. "Did you see Miss Scrimmage during the anthem? I thought she'd disintegrate!"

"I don't know," Boots said in a worried tone. "I still think The Fish knows about the flag . . . *and* the music . . . *and* the cat."

"How could he?" Bruno scoffed. "We were brilliant!"

His jubilation was interrupted by a knock at the door. Boots opened it and took a note from the office messenger. It read: *Bruno Walton and Melvin O'Neal are to present themselves at Mr. Sturgeon's office immediately following the dinner hour.*

Chapter 2

the fish's decree

Dinner wasn't too appetizing to Bruno and Boots, but they lingered over every morsel. Then, with no more excuse for delay, they walked down the marble corridor which led to the Headmaster's office.

Mrs. Davis, the school secretary, welcomed them with a sympathetic smile. "You boys played well today," she said kindly.

"Thank you, Ma'am," said Boots. "Is Mr. Sturgeon in?"

"He's expecting you. Go right in." She indicated the heavy oak door with *HEADMASTER* lettered in gold. They entered. Mr. Sturgeon wordlessly motioned them to a wooden bench facing his desk. In his eighteen years as Headmaster of Macdonald Hall he had never been known to display a sense of humour. Bruno and Boots quickly noted that although he didn't look any more severe than usual, he certainly didn't look any kindlier.

Mr. Sturgeon leaned back in his black-leather swivel chair and silently regarded them. His silver-rimmed glasses accentuated the steel of his grey eyes. Finally he spoke. "If you two put half the amount of effort into your studies that you spend getting into trouble, it is entirely possible that you would be the most brilliant students in the school."

Bruno and Boots sat frozen in silence.

"Since you entered this school last year, I have never been able to prove you guilty of anything. Yet guilty you are. Today you have set an infamous record! If I had any concrete proof that you switched the flag, or changed the music, or abducted the cat, I would be addressing your parents at this very moment."

The boys sat stiff and silent as statues.

"Now," Mr. Sturgeon continued, "*did* you do any of those things?"

"I guess it sort of looks that way, sir," Bruno murmured.

"*Which* of those things did you do?"

"All of them, sir," Bruno admitted.

"Yes. I suspected as much . . . Have you any idea what havoc you caused today?"

"We didn't mean any harm," Boots said.

"You didn't mean any harm," Mr. Sturgeon repeated almost sadly. "Did you not see the embarrassment we suffered in front of the spectators because of that ridiculous flag of — of — "

"Malbonia," Bruno supplied quietly.

"Did you not see how upset everyone was at the profaning of our national anthem? And to win a hockey game by demoralizing your opponents — by abducting their mascot! I cannot tell you the deep sense of shame I feel over the events of this day."

Mr. Sturgeon rose and began to pace back and forth in front of the bench.

"I have thought and thought about you ever since you began your — er — extra-curricular activities, and I believe that I have arrived at a solution which may save us all. There is a great deal of mischief in both of you, but I believe that you, Walton, are setting a bad example for O'Neal here. I have therefore decided to break up your partnership. You will both proceed to your room, pack your belongings and say goodbye to each other. From this point on, you are forbidden to associate in any manner whatsoever."

The boys sat stunned by this fatal message. Over the year their friendship had grown so vital to them that neither could imagine the thought of living without the other. No more shared jokes, no more moral support, no more comfortably messy room . . . no more Bruno and Boots!

"Walton," continued Mr. Sturgeon, "you will report to Dormitory 2, room 201, where you will share accommodation with Elmer Drimsdale."

Oh, no! Bruno thought. *The school ghoul!*

"And you, O'Neal, I have placed with George Wexford-Smyth III. Dormitory 1, room 109."

Oh no! Boots winced. *Moneybags piled to the ceiling!*

"You are dismissed," Mr. Sturgeon concluded. "I expect you to be settled in your new quarters by lights-out."

*   *   *

When Bruno and Boots had left the office, Mr. Sturgeon buzzed his secretary. "Mrs. Davis, please get me Mr. Hartley at York Academy."

"Yes, sir," she said. "He'll be glad to hear from you. He called five times during dinner. Seemed quite upset."

Mr. Sturgeon lit an expensive cigar and settled back in his chair to await the call. It came almost immediately.

"Hello, Hartley. Sturgeon here. I understand you've been calling . . . I say there, Hartley, could you speak a little more quietly? . . . Yes, that's much better . . . My dear Hartley, our boys did *not* take your cat. She merely hid on the bus to have her kittens . . . Now surely you're joking. The cat doesn't *skate*, after all . . . Well, that's out of my hands, Hartley. You'll have to take that up with Miss Scrimmage. Good evening."

He hung up and sat back, puffing triumphantly on the cigar. Mr. Sturgeon did not often smoke cigars — only when he was celebrating something.

*   *   *

Bruno and Boots riffled half-heartedly through their belongings, wasting as much time as possible. Every few minutes one of them would toss something into an open suitcase on his bed. Neither had spoken since they had left Mr. Sturgeon's office.

"Don't pack those socks," Bruno snapped suddenly.

"Why not?"

"Because they're mine."

"Oh." Boots tossed the socks across the room.

"We'll have to meet," Bruno said after a while.

"The Fish says we're not allowed," Boots reminded him.

"The Fish says! The Fish says!" Bruno mimicked. "The Fish has said enough for one day. I'll see you at midnight. The bushes behind the cannon."

"Midnight? What if I fall asleep?"

"Impossible. You'll be awake all night listening to the *clink-clink-clink* of George Wexford-Smyth III counting his money," Bruno growled. "Be there."

Nothing else was said. Shortly after nine the boys took a last fond look at their former home, shook hands solemnly and went their separate ways.

* * *

Bruno paused a moment before knocking at the door of room 201. It was opened by a tall, skinny boy with a crewcut. He wore a white shirt, black tie and grey flannel slacks. Thick glasses gave him the look of an owl.

"Elmer Drimsdale? Hi. I'm Bruno Walton," said Bruno, strolling in and setting down his suitcase. "Hey, an ant!" he exclaimed, stomping on it.

"You killed her!" Elmer shrieked. "You killed her! She was the queen of my whole colony!"

"You keep *ants*?" Bruno asked in disbelief.

"Yes," the boy replied. "I'm an entomologist. My world is the insect world."

Bruno nodded understandingly. "I always thought you were a bit buggy, Elmer. Which bed is mine? And kindly keep your ants out of it!"

"That one." Elmer pointed to the bed by the window. "But where am I going to get another queen for my colony?" he wailed.

Bruno shrugged. "Why don't you try spreading a little sugar around?" Then noticing Elmer's face he added,

"Hey, listen, I'm sorry. I didn't know it was your — uh — pet. I hope you find another one."

"Thank you," said Elmer reproachfully.

Bruno sighed and pulled off his sweater. "Boy, am I bushed. I'm going to take a bath and hit the sack early." He started towards the bathroom.

"No!" Elmer shouted. "You'll kill my specimens!" Bruno stopped in mid-step and stared at him.

"My goldfish! They laid eggs in the bathtub today."

"Congratulations," muttered Bruno. "I know a cat that had kittens today too. Do I get to know the reason for this aquarium in the bathroom?"

"I'm studying the crossbreeding of goldfish," Elmer explained. "I'm an ichthyologist. My world is the undersea world."

Bruno struggled, unwashed, into his pyjamas. "I always thought you were a bit fishy, Elmer," he groaned.

He crawled into his new bed. It was exactly the same as his old one, but it felt strange and uncomfortable. The whole room was the same, really, even the dull cream-beige paint on the walls. But it didn't *feel* the same. Maybe it was because of the posters. His old room had been plastered with movie posters, one crude enough it would have been confiscated by the teachers had it not been safely hidden away during dormitory inspections. Elmer's idea of artistic wall decoration was a labelled diagram of the Pacific salmon.

Bruno sighed. Seven hundred kids in this school, he thought wearily, and I have to get stuck with Jacques Cousteau!

* * *

15

Boots knocked on the door of room 109. It was opened by a handsome fellow dressed in several hundred dollars' worth of suede and cashmere sports clothes. His haircut, Boots noted, was the hundred-dollar stylist variety.

"Yes? What is it?" the youth queried.

"Mr. Sturgeon sent me," said Boots. "I'm your new roommate, Boots O'Neal."

Very reluctantly he was invited inside. "Boots?" said the boy with disgust. "What kind of a name is Boots? What is your *real* name? Nicknames are so vulgar."

"My *real* name is Melvin," replied Boots grimly, "but nobody calls me that. *Nobody*."

"How do you do. I am George Wexford-Smyth III. You may have the bed by the window. I never sleep near a window. The night air is bad for my sinuses."

Boots, who always slept with the window wide open, said nothing. He sat on the edge of his new bed and surveyed the room: it reminded him of his Grade 8 field trip to the Toronto Stock Exchange. Financial charts covered the walls almost like wallpaper. His roommate was standing staring at one of these charts as though the end of the world were at hand.

"Something wrong, George?"

"My Magneco," George announced tragically. "It's gone down three points and lost me a small fortune."

"Oh," said Boots, beginning to unpack. He carried his toothbrush, toothpaste and soap into the bathroom, but emerged a few seconds later with a puzzled look on his face. "What is that drugstore doing in the bathroom?"

"Those are my medicines," George huffed. "Better safe than sorry. You never know when disease may strike."

"Oh," said Boots again. Because the shelves were over-flowing with inhalers, nasal sprays, pain killers, cold tablets, tranquillizers, laxatives and antibiotics, he was going to have to store his own toiletries in his dressing gown pocket.

Climbing resignedly into bed, Boots reflected that if only Bruno were there the room would be paradise. It was completely wired with the most expensive sound equipment, and the sixty-inch flat-screen TV pulled in 750 channels via a mini-satellite dish perched on the windowsill. Besides, he thought with a grin, they wouldn't have to worry about illness: even if they caught elephantiasis, he was positive George had a cure somewhere in that bathroom.

* * *

In the Headmaster's residence Mr. Sturgeon suddenly sat bolt upright in bed. "Now where on earth," he exclaimed, "did they manage to find the flag of Malbonia?"

Chapter 3

the cannon at midnight

Boots rose from his bed and silently checked George's solid-gold Rolex watch. Ten minutes to twelve. He had to hurry if he was going to be on time to meet Bruno. He scrambled into his dressing gown and eased the window open.

"Shut the window . . . pneumonia . . . " groaned George in his sleep.

Boots climbed onto the sill and made the short drop to the ground. Crouching beside the building, he scanned the deserted campus. All clear so far. Keeping low and in the shadows, he stole towards the meeting place on the south lawn. He slipped into the bushes behind the cannon and whispered, "Bruno?"

No answer. No Bruno.

Five long minutes passed. Boots had been nervous to

start with, but now he was really worried. A few more minutes went by. He checked his own twenty-dollar watch. It had stopped at quarter past nine.

Must be an omen, Boots thought, wrapping his cold feet in the tail of his dressing gown. *That was when Bruno and I left our room.*

A rustling in the bushes startled him. "Bruno?" he whispered. "What took you so long?"

When a fat brown jackrabbit burst from the woods and scampered across the lawn into the darkness, Boots drooped in despair. Suddenly a familiar voice chuckled, "Aha! Talking to a rabbit, eh?"

"Where have you been?" Boots snapped. "I've been sitting here scared stiff!"

"Well," Bruno shrugged, "I thought we might be a bit hungry, so I stopped off at the kitchen and got us a little snack." He held out a huge brown bag. "Care for a sandwich?"

He spread the contents of the bag between them. There was a loaf of bread, an entire delicatessen of cold meats, a package of sliced cheese, four apples, six oranges and two containers of chocolate milk.

Boots whistled admiringly. "Boy, with all this we could run away from school." Then he added wistfully, "And that's just what I feel like doing."

"That bad?" asked Bruno, slapping meat and cheese between two slices of bread.

"Worse!" exclaimed Boots. "You wouldn't believe it." He bit sadly into an apple. "George Wexford-Smyth III is a crackpot! The room is full of medicines and stock exchange charts. I can't keep my stuff in the bathroom because of all his pills and ointments, and I can't hang up my posters because the stock charts take up too much room."

"At least he isn't an ichthyologist whose world is the undersea world," Bruno countered. "Our bathtub is full of caviar. The ichthyologist is studying the crossbreeding of goldfish, and I am doomed never to have a bath again as long as I live with Elmer Drimsdale — and that won't be too long if I have anything to say about it."

Boots sighed. "That's just it. Unfortunately we have *nothing* to say about it."

"Well, we'll just have to *do* something, then," decided Bruno. "So he's really as heavy into stocks as they say?"

"Scout's honour," said Boots, saluting. "I was just dropping off to sleep tonight when the big financier got a message from his broker. Magneco went down another two points. George is wiped out."

"Oh, that's nothing," Bruno replied bitterly. "At least you've got just one roommate to put up with. I have about a thousand and I've already killed one — too bad it wasn't Elmer."

"Huh? What are you talking about?" Boots asked.

"Ants," said Bruno. "A metropolis of ants. Elmer is an entomologist. His world is the insect world."

"He keeps *ants*?" Boots asked in disbelief.

Bruno nodded. "He not only keeps them; he exercises them. His queen was out for a stroll when I scrunched her."

"What are we going to do?" Boots wailed. "I don't think I can put up with another minute of George swallowing pills, gargling and spraying his nose. He won't let me open a window because of his sinuses and he wants to call me Melvin because nicknames are so vulgar!" He gestured despairingly with both hands, then reached for a slice of bread.

"Elmer's not really such a bad guy," mumbled Bruno with his mouth full, "but he sure isn't for me. Come to think of it, he isn't really for anybody — except maybe his ants and his goldfish. By the way, did I mention the fish tank? It bubbles day and night." He yawned. "Listen, Boots, it's getting late. Between the two of us we should be able to figure some way out of this mess. Meet me here the same time tomorrow night."

"Right," answered Boots. "Hey, what'll we do with the rest of this food?"

Bruno stuffed the leftovers into the bag. "I'll shove it in the cannon," he decided. "Then we'll have an emergency supply."

"Just remember," Boots prodded, "you're always bragging that you have an answer for everything. This time you've got to deliver! We've *got* to find a way to ditch these guys and get back together again!"

"Don't worry," Bruno promised. "I'll think of something — Melvin."

"Very funny," Boots growled. "Goodnight."

"'Night."

A corner of the lunch bag, sticking out of the cannon's mouth, flapped silently in the darkness.

Chapter 4

assignment: obnoxious!

By the time Boots awoke the next morning George had already returned from breakfast. He was examining the morning paper and checking his charts, making adjustments with a red pen.

"Morning," Boots murmured. "How's Magneco?"

"Recovering, recovering," George said briskly, as though he had no time for small talk.

Boots, a notorious morning sneezer, rattled off four violent *achoos!* in a row. Immediately George whipped out a disinfectant and began to spray the entire room, giving special attention to Boots' bed. "Germs!" he cried in a panic. "You didn't tell me you had a cold! I would have put up my screen!"

Boots stared, first amused and then disgusted, as George wheeled out a large screen and placed it between the two beds. On Boots' side was a sign that said *QUARANTINE*.

"Cut it out," Boots protested. "I haven't got a cold. I always sneeze in the morning when I wake up." Reluctantly George put away the screen.

"I'll take your word for it," he said. "But sneezing *does* spread germs, you know. You ought to keep a paper bag beside your bed and every morning you can sneeze into it and put it out with the trash to be burned."

Boots started to insist on his right to sneeze anywhere he wanted, but then gave up and began to get dressed. Before he was finished George had turned from his charts, picked up an armload of books and headed for his first class of the day, advanced economics. A few minutes later Boots set out for his math class, but not before making a point of coughing on George's pillow.

Boots was in a foul mood. He knew that Bruno was going to be in that class too, and that they would not even be allowed to say hello to one another. His world had become a very uncomfortable place.

* * *

Elmer's alarm shrilled at the usual 6 AM. Bruno managed to open one eye and was vaguely aware of a headache. "What time is it?" he mumbled.

"It is exactly six o'clock," Elmer said.

"AM?" Bruno cried in dismay.

"You bet," Elmer said brightly. "There's lots of work to be done before breakfast."

"Like what?" Bruno snarled. It was his habit to miss breakfast, sleep until quarter to nine, then make a frantic effort to get washed and dressed and to his first class on time.

"I have to check on my goldfish experiment," Elmer explained, "and make some notes. Then I have several other experiments to tend to, and my ants to take care of."

Bruno sat up, swung his legs over the side of the bed, then paused. "Is it safe to stand on the floor?" he asked. "I wouldn't want to step on anybody important."

"Oh, perfectly safe," said Elmer. "They're still sleeping."

"That proves they've got more brains than we have, Elmer, but since I'm awake I may as well unpack." Bruno heaved his suitcase onto the bed and threw it open. He went over to the large dresser and pulled out the bottom drawer. "This one mine?"

"No-o-o!"

Bruno was frozen by Elmer's anguished scream. He stared down into the drawer. Lining the bottom were dozens of tiny pots of earth with little plants sprouting in them.

"You've ruined my experiment!" Elmer wailed. "Those plants were supposed to be in total darkness for a hundred and forty-four hours. Now I'll have to start all over!"

"What do you have plants in a drawer for?" Bruno asked.

"I am a botanist," Elmer explained. "My world is the world of plants."

"I always thought you were a bit earthy, Elmer," Bruno grunted, "but this is too much. Just where do I get to keep my underwear?"

"Couldn't you keep it in your suitcase for the next six days?" Elmer pleaded.

24

"Oh, all right," Bruno agreed. "Anything for you, Elmer."

Washed, dressed and at least half awake, Bruno arrived at the dining room for his first breakfast ever at Macdonald Hall. Wearily he picked up a tray and walked over to where two elderly women in white uniforms were dishing out breakfast.

"Look, Martha," one said, "a new boy." She turned to Bruno. "Welcome to Macdonald Hall, dear. When did you arrive?"

The other boys being served hooted loudly.

"This is my second year," Bruno grinned sheepishly. "I guess I'm just not much for breakfast."

But unaccustomed as he was to eating early, he quickly managed to put away three scrambled eggs, six strips of bacon, four large pancakes with maple syrup, two pieces of toast and three glasses of milk. "It's a good thing you don't come to breakfast too often," one student observed as Bruno was downing the last of his milk. "They'd have to raise the fees just to feed you."

Bruno patted his stomach. "That was delicious. You know, I may even come again sometime."

As he entered math class, he noted that Boots was already there, sitting as far away from his usual place as possible without actually being outside the room. He also found that he was incapable of giving his friend the usual smile of greeting, forbidden or not. Breakfast was sitting very heavily on his stomach; he felt sick.

The geometry class was a horrendous experience for both of them. Bruno was trying to keep his spirits up and his breakfast down, and Boots was yawning hugely. So the teacher was confronted on one side with Bruno's green face, and on the other with Boots' gaping mouth.

"Are we keeping you up, O'Neal?" he finally demanded.

"Sorry, sir," said Boots. "I was up late last night. I guess I'm pretty tired."

The teacher turned to Bruno. "I think you should have stayed in bed this morning, Walton. You don't look at all well."

"Oh, it's nothing, sir," replied Bruno. "I just ate too much breakfast."

A boy in the front row turned around. "Breakfast? *You*?"

"That will do," said the teacher. "Walton, I'm sending you back to bed. Here is your authorization." He scribbled a few words on a piece of paper and handed it over. Bruno was more than happy to obey.

* * *

Boots sat in a corner of the dining room munching on a sandwich. News of Mr. Sturgeon's order had spread. Boots' friends, sensing that he was in a grim mood, left him alone, although five of them sat conspicuously at a table for six with one chair pulled out invitingly in case he chose to join them. He didn't.

He was very much aware that Bruno had not come to lunch. He must be sick, really sick, Boots thought. And a lot Elmer Drimsdale was going to care!

* * *

Bruno spent most of the day in bed, although as soon as his mammoth breakfast had settled he felt considerably better. He lay there thinking. Elmer hates me, he mused cheerfully. I'd like to booby-trap one of his experiments, but that would just make him mad. He'd probably complain to The Fish . . .

26

Instantly an amazing plan sprouted in Bruno's fertile mind, one he was later to call his "glorious idea."

He was still in bed when Elmer came in at four o'clock. "Are you still sick?" his roommate asked solicitously.

"Sort of," Bruno answered, touched by Elmer's concern and a little ashamed of his earlier thoughts and plans.

"Gee, that's swell!" Elmer rummaged through a large crate which stood beside his desk and produced a high-magnification microscope and a box of glass slides. "I'd like to study your germs," he explained. "Would you mind coughing on this slide?"

"Yes, I would mind very much," Bruno growled. "Why?"

"I'm a microbiologist," Elmer answered. "My world is the microbe world."

"I always thought you were very small, Elmer," said Bruno wearily. "Go away."

Elmer mumbled something about lack of co-operation and reluctantly put away his equipment.

"Oh, don't take it so hard, Elmer," Bruno reassured him. "Maybe some day I'll catch something really good and then I'll let you culture it."

"Really and truly?" Elmer asked hopefully.

"Really and truly," replied Bruno, "I promise to do my very best to get some terrible disease."

He watched as his roommate made the rounds of his experiments. Carefully and lovingly Elmer restarted the plant experiment and shut the bottom drawer of the dresser, reminding Bruno that he had only a hundred and forty-four more hours to live out of his suitcase. The ants had completed an entire new tunnel, and he rewarded them with a spoonful of sugar. Everything was going along swimmingly in the bathtub, although no fry had hatched yet, but the fish tank was not quite so serene.

"My algae eater!" Elmer exclaimed. "He's dead!"

"Maybe it was something he ate," Bruno suggested. "Look how sick I got from having breakfast."

"Have you been near this tank?" Elmer asked suspiciously.

"I haven't even *looked* in its direction," Bruno defended himself. "Fish are not my idea of a good time — unless they're dipped in batter and served with french fries."

"I guess I cleaned the tank too thoroughly," Elmer decided, "and didn't leave him enough food. Poor devil."

Bruno rolled over, turned his face to the wall and switched on his portable radio. "No, no!" Elmer cried.

"What *now*?"

"Turn that off this instant! The noise is bad for my plants!"

"Your plants are closed up in the drawer!" Bruno yelled. "They can't even hear it!"

"Not *those* plants — *these* plants." Elmer swept open the curtains to reveal a triple row of pots on the window sill.

"I see," sighed Bruno, and switched off his radio — more determined than ever that Elmer had to go.

* * *

When Boots returned from classes he found George on his hands and knees washing the room with alcohol. "Good, you're back," said George. "Watch carefully, please. Next week it will be your turn for sterilizing duty. It has to be done every second day."

"What do you wash?" Boots asked in amazement,

28

wrinkling his nose from the strong odour.

"Everything," George replied.

"Ceiling? Walls?" asked Boots. "Furniture?"

"And everything else," George added.

"What happens if I want to smoke in this fire trap?"

"*Smoke*?" George cried. "Smoking is hazardous to your health! I absolutely forbid it! Besides, it's against the rules. You wouldn't dare."

Boots, who had never smoked in his life, thought of taking it up just to irritate George. "All right," he said when his anger had cooled. "Your idea of sterilizing the room is terrific. *You* do it." He strode to the window and threw it wide, stifling George's cry of protest with a look that would have melted steel. "It stinks in here," he said bluntly, and sat down at his desk to do his homework.

After a while George said, "May I please shut the window? It's getting very chilly."

Boots, who was freezing but not ready to admit it, replied, "Certainly. I wouldn't want you to catch pneumonia."

That was the end of their conversation for the rest of the evening.

* * *

Boots arrived at the cannon ten minutes early, to find Bruno already there. "All right, Bruno, this is it!" he declared. "Either you come up with an idea tonight or I go A.W.O.L.! The Third is driving me nuts!" He proceeded to describe in detail the fine points of sterilizing duty. "And this morning when I sneezed — you know how I sneeze when I wake up — he sprayed the room and put a quarantine screen up to isolate me. I just can't stand any more!"

"Shh! Stop yelling," Bruno whispered. "The old Walton brain came through. I have developed a glorious idea. Are you with me?"

"I'll do *anything!*" Boots vowed. "Tell me."

Bruno left the cover of the bushes to retrieve their bag of food from the cannon. They sat down together and began to chew on some dried-out bread.

"It's really very simple," Bruno said. "George and Elmer don't like us very much. But what if they hated us? I mean really hated us — enough to go to The Fish and complain about us?"

"What good would that do?" Boots protested. "We'd just get into more trouble."

"Now stop and think," said Bruno. "The Fish is punishing us, not them. They're the two best little boys in the whole school. If they demand to be rid of us, The Fish is bound to give in. And where does that leave us?"

"Chained to the office wall, probably," Boots muttered.

"Well, have you got a better idea?" Bruno demanded.

"No," Boots admitted glumly.

"Well then, this is it — starting tomorrow we make ourselves so obnoxious that good old George and sweet little Elmer will run screaming to The Fish to complain."

Chapter 5

you keep ants?

Once again Elmer's alarm went off with an ear-splitting shrill at 6 AM. He rose promptly and began to dress, vaguely aware that something was not quite right. He puzzled over the odd feeling, but continued to get dressed.

"My ants!" he cried suddenly. "My ants are gone!"

Elmer stared at Bruno's bed. It was empty. It did not take him long to realize that Bruno's absence and the ants' disappearance were somehow related. He threw the door open and bolted into the hall.

About three doors away, Bruno was hurrying along with the large glass aquarium that contained Elmer's ant colony.

"What are you doing?" Elmer shrieked.

"Haven't you ever seen *Born Free*?" Bruno replied. "These poor creatures are in captivity. They deserve to be free."

"No!"

The racket was beginning to penetrate into the other rooms. Scrambling noises and cries of, "Hey, pipe down!" and "What the heck is going on out there?" could be heard all along the corridor.

"Freedom is their right," Bruno continued solemnly. "Go, go, little ants. The wide world awaits you." On that note, he dumped the contents of the aquarium onto the floor.

Elmer's face wrinkled up like that of a baby about to bawl. If Bruno hadn't been sure that he was doing something absolutely necessary, he would have felt terribly guilty.

Suddenly the door of room 205 burst open and hit the mess on the floor. Sand and ants flew all over the hall. Elmer let out a piercing scream.

"What did I do? What did I do?" asked Perry Elbert. "I just came out to see what was going on!"

"I'm going to see Mr. Sturgeon!" Elmer raged.

Perry was dumbfounded. "Please don't," he pleaded. "I didn't mean to open the door!"

From room 203 a shoe came flying into the hall. "Shut up out there!" yelled a voice. "It's only six-thirty!"

"They're getting away!" Elmer wailed. It was true. Ants were scurrying in every direction.

"What's going on?" asked a sleepy voice from 211.

"Stampede!" Bruno yelled. By this time he was enjoying himself immensely.

"All I did was open the door . . . " Perry kept insisting.

More doors opened. In seconds every boy in Dormitory 2 was milling around in the general confusion. The hub-bub was broken by Elmer's half-crazed voice. "Everyone stop!" he commanded. "Don't move! You'll step on my ants!"

"You keep ants?" echoed a dozen voices.

"He's an entomologist," Bruno intoned. "His world is the insect world."

"Help me!" Elmer pleaded. "Help me get them back into the aquarium!"

"*Born free*," sang Bruno, "*as free as the wind blows . . .*"

In a short time a gang of pyjama-clad boys were crawling around the halls after Elmer's ants, using water glasses, toothbrush containers and even test tubes to collect them in.

"Elmer, Elmer, here's three!"

"We've uncovered a whole bunch of them under the radiator!"

"Here, Elmer, here's nine or ten."

"Elmer, Elmer, there's a crack in the floor and they're going in there by the hundreds!"

"Be careful, stupid, you just stepped on one!"

"Elmer, about fifty have run up the wall and they're going out the window!"

"Yecch!"

"Report nine dead in room 213. Arthur has a chameleon and he's eating them!"

"*Who's* clumsy? You stepped on *three!*"

When the dust settled, about fifty ants were present and accounted for; another thirty were proven dead. The rest, some five hundred and twenty, were still at large.

As the boys settled back to normal and began to dress for breakfast, Perry walked over to Elmer. "I only opened the door," he implored. "I don't even understand the bit about the ants."

* * *

At 7:30 that same morning Boots was writing to his mother. George was still asleep.

Dear Mom, Boots scribbled. *How are you? I'm fine.*

He hated writing letters, but his parents expected to hear from him once a week. And it had to be a real, old-fashioned handwritten letter. No e-mail for Mom and Dad. They were stuck in the Stone Age. *Everything is okay. I have a new roommate. He is rich and a crackpot, but with him I will never get sick. Your loving son, Melvin.*

Boots watched George intently for a few seconds to be sure he was sound asleep. Then, on tiptoe, he approached the only shelf in the room that was not filled with medicines. Carefully he took down the book marked MINT STAMPS — CANADA and opened it up. A set of Queen Victoria 1886 definitives caught his eye. He removed three stamps and left the book open on George's desk. After neatly arranging a few coins on the open page, he stuck the stamps on the envelope and mailed the letter on his way to breakfast. He had never felt so rotten in his whole life.

Boots joined his friends in the dining room, hoping the company would help him forget what he had just done. But he didn't take part in their chatter; instead he sat wondering about Bruno's first attack on Elmer. Bruno can't possibly be putting Elmer through what George is going to suffer, he decided.

Just then the peace and quiet of the dining room was shattered by the half-demented voice of George Wexford-Smyth III. "Where is he?"

George charged into the dining hall in his pyjamas; Boots dropped his fork with a clatter. "AHA! There you are!" George screamed. "You dirty rotten cad! Where are my stamps?"

"I borrowed some to mail a letter," Boots replied offhandedly, trying to keep cool.

"You stuck them on a *letter*?" George cried. "You've ruined them!"

"What's all the fuss about?" Boots asked. "I left you enough money to cover them."

"Enough money!" George's face grew purple. "Those three stamps are worth seven hundred dollars!"

Boots pretended to be astonished. "Seven hundred dollars?" he scoffed. "They added up to less than a buck." He spoke with amazing nonchalance.

Growling something about seeing the Headmaster, George Wexford-Smyth III wheeled and tore out of the dining room.

* * *

Bruno smiled when he received the summons from Mr. Sturgeon. His plan was obviously right on schedule. He was still humming *Born Free* as he walked to the office. Mrs. Davis greeted him with her usual sympathetic smile and sent him right in.

Mr. Sturgeon was waiting for him. So was Elmer Drimsdale. Elmer's face wore a smug now-you're-going-to-get-it expression.

"You are familiar with the bench, Walton," said Mr.

Sturgeon. "Sit down, please." Bruno sat down on the hard wooden bench, noting that Elmer was comfortably established in the padded visitor's chair. "Drimsdale tells me that you have destroyed his valuable ant colony. Is that true?"

"Well, I guess so, sir," Bruno answered. "You see, I was trying to set them free. All my life I've hated circuses and zoos . . . anywhere animals are held in captivity."

"Those are very fine feelings," said the Headmaster, "but they are your own. The ant colony, however, was not your own: it was Drimsdale's. I think you owe him an apology."

"I'm sorry, Elmer," Bruno said readily. Elmer did not reply.

"That's fine," said Mr. Sturgeon. "And now I think you owe him something else."

Bruno waited silently. Mr. Sturgeon leaned back in his chair and tapped his fingers together. "Drimsdale, how many ants did you have in that colony?"

"Six hundred, sir," Elmer answered. "And now I've got fifty."

"Walton," said Mr. Sturgeon, "how is your arithmetic? What is fifty from six hundred?"

Bruno's heart sank. He swallowed hard. "Five hundred and fifty, sir."

"Very good. That is the exact number of ants that I expect you to collect, together with new sand for the aquarium, by the end of the week."

"Me, sir?" Bruno asked. "Alone? By *myself*, sir? With no one to help me?"

"You catch on quickly," Mr. Sturgeon replied. "That will

be all. I suggest you begin immediately: five hundred and fifty is a lot of ants."

"Yes, sir," said Bruno. He rose to leave. Just as his hand touched the doorknob, the Headmaster spoke again.

"Oh, Walton, one more thing. I have been forced to call an exterminator to spray Dormitory 2. The cost will be deducted from your spending money."

"Yes, sir," Bruno repeated, and escaped from the office. He was no longer singing. Then and only then did it dawn on him that neither Mr. Sturgeon nor Elmer had mentioned the riot that had taken place in the dormitory hall. Elmer, in dire distress over the loss of his ants, had simply not noticed the ruckus.

As he walked through the outer office, Bruno saw George Wexford-Smyth III, white-faced and tight-lipped, waiting to see the Headmaster. I wonder what Boots did? he thought.

* * *

With the note from Mrs. Davis in his hand, Boots crossed the campus on his way to Mr. Sturgeon's office. As he approached the flagpole in front of the Faculty Building he suddenly caught sight of Bruno — on his hands and knees in the grass, surrounded by jars and boxes, spreading sugar on an anthill.

"Come out, come out, wherever you are," Bruno was chanting. "Uncle Bruno will take you to a new home with your wicked Uncle Elmer, where you can dig tunnels until you drop dead."

"Hey," Boots hissed, "what *are* you doing?"

"It's quite obvious what I'm doing," Bruno grumbled. "I'm finding the five hundred and fifty ants I owe Elmer. What are you doing?"

"I'm on my way to see The Fish too," Boots said uneasily. "George finked."

"What did you do?" Bruno asked.

"Mailed a letter." Looking very unhappy, Boots walked on.

"Sometimes I just don't understand him," Bruno muttered, daintily picking up an ant.

Boots walked through the big oak doors of the Faculty Building and proceeded down the corridor to the office. Mrs. Davis was still wearing her sympathetic smile. She sent him right in.

"Bench," snapped Mr. Sturgeon, pointing to the seat across from his desk. Like Elmer before him, George was seated in the visitor's chair.

"O'Neal," Mr. Sturgeon began, "I hear that you have ruined three valuable stamps that belonged to Wexford-Smyth."

"But I paid for them, sir," Boots defended himself.

"Yes," Mr. Sturgeon said, "you paid for them. You paid a few coins when in reality they were worth seven hundred dollars."

"But, sir," Boots protested, "they were just sitting there. I didn't want to wake George up, and the letter to my mother was late, so I just — "

"I know what you 'just,'" Mr. Sturgeon interrupted. "Now, see here, O'Neal. You cannot *possibly* expect me to believe that you thought those were ordinary stamps. One need not be a philatelist to know the difference between Queen Victoria and Queen Elizabeth II. I think you owe Wexford-Smyth an apology."

Boots studied the carpet. "I'm sorry, George," he mumbled.

"And I think you also owe him seven hundred dollars."

Boots' head jerked up. "But sir! Where am I going to get seven hundred dollars?"

"Washing dishes," replied Mr. Sturgeon. "After school, from seven till nine. The school will pay you five dollars an hour."

"But, sir!" Boots exclaimed. "That's three whole months!"

"Quite correct," said Mr. Sturgeon. "That will be all, O'Neal. You are dismissed."

As he crossed the campus and passed Bruno, Boots muttered, "Well, I'm ahead seven hundred to five-fifty."

"What are you talking about?" Bruno growled.

"I got three months of dishwashing," Boots snarled, "at five dollars an hour!"

"What did you *do*?"

"I told you," Boots snapped. "I mailed a letter."

Chapter 6

round two

The window of room 201 opened silently and a shadowy figure climbed out and dropped to the ground. Bruno crept around the edge of the deserted campus, across the dark highway and over the wrought-iron fence that surrounded Miss Scrimmage's Finishing School for Young Ladies. Beside the residence building he picked up a handful of pebbles and tossed them at a second-floor window.

After a few moments the window opened and a familiar head appeared. "Bruno? . . . Is that you?" a voice whispered.

"Who else?" said Bruno. "Listen, I have to borrow Petunia for a couple of days."

"What for?"

"I have to get rid of a friend," Bruno replied. "Can you get her down to me?"

"Give me a couple of minutes."

Bruno waited. Finally a cage appeared in the window and began to dangle slowly towards the ground, suspended by a leather belt, three pairs of panty hose, one bathrobe belt and the bathrobe itself.

"Got it," whispered Bruno. "Thanks, Diane."

"Don't mention it. Just don't forget to feed her."

"What does she eat?" Bruno asked.

"This," the girl replied. A bag of Mi-Choice Skunk Chow sailed out of the window and clunked Bruno on the head. *Women!* he thought in disgust.

With the caged skunk under one arm and the skunk food in the other, he made his way to Macdonald Hall and into his room. After hiding Petunia under his bed, he changed Elmer's alarm clock to his own customary rising hour — 8:45 — and fell asleep.

*   *   *

Although it was well after midnight, a dim light still shone in the print shop. Boots and the editor of the school newspaper were labouring over the press. A single sheet of newsprint lay before them.

"I'll tear it out," Boots said, "so it'll look as if it's from a real newspaper."

"Is there really such a disease as creeping caliotis?" the editor asked.

"I hope not," grinned Boots. "Awful, isn't it?"

"Sure is. What are you going to do with the clipping?"

"It's for a hypochondriac friend of mine," Boots explained. "By the time I get through with him, he'll be a basket case. Thanks a lot for your help."

"Any time . . . I pity your friend, though."

"I don't," Boots replied grimly.

* * *

"It's quarter to *nine*!" screamed Elmer, bounding out of bed and hitting his head on the wall. "Who changed my alarm clock?"

"I did," said Bruno, dressing rapidly. "It's about time you learned to get up at a civilized hour."

"But what about breakfast? I'll starve! What about classes? I've never been late in my life! What will they do to me?"

"If you're five minutes late, you get a detention," Bruno explained gravely. "If you're ten minutes late, it's the rack."

At 8:55 Elmer flew out of the room with his shirt tails flapping, his belt dangling and his shoelaces untied. He was unwashed and uncombed — but he had five minutes to spare.

As soon as Elmer had gone, Bruno reached under his bed, pulled out the cage and opened the door. "Good morning, Petunia. I trust you slept well. How about some breakfast?"

Ignoring the food, Petunia stepped daintily around the room examining her surroundings.

"So okay, no breakfast. I've got to go to class now anyway," said Bruno. "Be a good girl, Petunia — and when Elmer comes in, scare the living daylights out of him!"

* * *

At first light Boots began to put his plan into action. He checked the phony newspaper article before putting it into his desk drawer. *Large red spots*. Boots took a small paper bag from under his pillow. It contained a brush and a jar of poster paint. With great care he began to dab red spots on the face of his sleeping roommate. He examined his handiwork, silently congratulated himself and went back to bed. When he opened his eyes again at eight, George was just waking up.

"George, what's wrong with you?" Boots cried.

George turned pale. "Wh–what do you mean?" he stammered.

"There are big red spots all over your face! See for yourself." Boots motioned towards the mirror.

George looked at his reflection and shrieked. "What is it? What is it?"

Boots gasped. "Omigosh! I think I know!" He opened his drawer, dug around in the contents and finally drew out the newspaper article. "This was in Thursday's *Star* — my mother sent it to me. Listen!" He began to read:

"*Creeping caliotis, a rare tropical disease, has killed nine people in Toronto within the last thirty-six hours. The disease is believed to have come to Canada through imported livestock and is highly contagious. Major symptoms are large red spots scattered over the facial area, followed by shortness of breath, then head, throat and chest pains.*"

Right on cue George began to puff. "I'm having shortness of breath!" he gasped. "I ache all over! *I've got creeping caliotis!* Get me to the infirmary right away!"

"No, don't move!" Boots cried. "Listen!" He continued to read: "*Chances of survival are drastically reduced if the victim attempts to move around. Complete bed rest is essential.*" Boots handed the clipping to George. "Read it for yourself," he said. "You'd better get back to bed right away."

George nodded and crept into his bed. The possibility that his life — though barely started — might soon be over stunned him.

"I'll get Dr. Leroy right away," Boots assured him. "But first — no offence, old boy — I think . . . " He wheeled out George's quarantine screen and placed it between the two beds, making sure the sign was on George's side.

"Creeping caliotis!" George moaned. "Tell the doctor to hurry!"

"I will," Boots promised. "But don't you move from that bed. You need complete bed rest or you've had it." Boots picked up his books and headed for class — leaving George at death's door.

* * *

At four that afternoon Bruno hurried to his room with a jar containing the last of the five hundred and fifty ants he owed Elmer. As he was about to open the door, a loud scream erupted from within, followed by an enormous crash. The door flew open and out shot Elmer, his expression wild, his nose bleeding. He ran full-tilt into Bruno, knocking him down and sending the jar of ants spiralling into the wall, where it shattered. Once again Dormitory 2 was crawling with insects.

"My ants!" Bruno shrieked, in perfect imitation of Elmer.

"Skunk!" cried Elmer. "What's a skunk doing in our room?"

Bruno had been waiting all day for that question. "I'm a skunkologist," he explained. "My world is the skunk world."

Elmer just stared at him. Then Petunia trotted out into the hall and Elmer screamed again.

"Stop that," warned Bruno. "If you upset her, she'll spray the whole place."

Elmer crouched behind Bruno and continued to scream as the skunk explored the hall.

"Shut up!" called a voice. "I'm trying to do my homework!"

A door opened and a boy peered out into the hall. "Oh, no! Ants!" he cried. "They're back! And this time they've brought a skunk with them!"

More doors opened. Soon dozens of boys were milling around.

"Ants!"

"Skunk!"

"Help!"

Bruno, worried that Petunia was going to be trampled in the riot, picked her up and carried her over to Elmer. "Here, Petunia," he said. "Kiss and make up. You weren't nice. You gave Uncle Elmer a nasty fright." Elmer backed away, trembling.

"Stand still!" Bruno ordered. "You'll step on my ants!"

"You keep ants *too*?" cried one boy. "201's a bughouse!"

"I had ninety-six ants in that jar," Bruno sternly informed Elmer. "You owe me ninety-six ants."

Only then did Bruno notice a familiar figure standing at the end of the hall, his arms folded, watching. Mr. Sturgeon spoke quietly, but every boy heard and obeyed. "All of you — into your rooms. Walton, give me that skunk."

Bruno held Petunia out to Mr. Sturgeon. She bit his

finger. "I'll get her cage, sir," Bruno said quickly. He went into his room, fished the cage out from under the bed and locked Petunia in. "Here she is, sir."

"You carry it," ordered Mr. Sturgeon. "And follow me. Unless I'm mistaken, this animal is the pet of a young lady at Miss Scrimmage's. I am not going to ask how it came into your possession because, frankly, I do not wish to know. But we will return it to its owner together."

* * *

Boots tiptoed into his room after classes. The light was dim and the victim lay still on his bed, looking paler than the sheets and apparently breathing his last.

"Where have you been?" George moaned. "Where's the doctor?"

"Brace yourself," Boots told him, tying a handkerchief around his face like a surgical mask. "Dr. Leroy has creeping caliotis too; so does three-quarters of the school. They're dropping like flies. It's a full-fledged epidemic!"

"Has anybody *died*?" George asked, terrified.

"Not yet," Boots replied gravely, "but there are lots in comas. The army has sent a medical unit and the campus is in quarantine. There's even a roadblock."

"But did you tell them about me?" George groaned.

Boots nodded. "Of course, but you're three hundred and fifty-second on the waiting list. Don't worry. I'll stay and take care of you until help comes."

George was overcome with gratitude. He reached for a paper and pencil on the night table. "I've been writing my will," he croaked, his throat obviously very sore. "I'm going to leave you my Magneco for your devotion, Melvin." He wrote a few lines and collapsed back onto the pillow.

"Could you get me a cold cloth for my head?" he pleaded. "I must have a terribly high fever."

Boots wet a washcloth and gently placed it on his roommate's forehead. "I'd better go and write my mother," he said sadly. "If I catch creeping caliotis from you I'll want her to have a last few words to remember me by."

"Ooooh!" groaned George. He raised a trembling hand to his forehead and picked up the wet cloth to rearrange it. Large red blobs covered the white terrycloth. He stared at it for a few seconds, then rubbed it across his cheek. More red blobs.

"Paint," said George softly; then louder, "Paint . . . You *tricked* me! *I'll kill you!*" He leaped out of bed, grabbed a cricket bat and tore after Boots, who by this time was out of the room and halfway out of the building.

* * *

Mr. Sturgeon, Bruno and Petunia were making their way across the campus when Boots flashed by. "Hello, sir!" he panted.

Seconds later a pyjama-clad George Wexford-Smyth III thundered by in hot pursuit, screaming and waving a cricket bat.

Bruno did not dare comment, but as they continued on their way, he distinctly heard Mr. Sturgeon murmur, "I hope he catches him."

Chapter 7

desperate measures

Bruno was getting impatient: Elmer was having real trouble falling asleep. How was he ever going to get out to see Boots? And he *had* to see Boots. The present strategy was getting them into more hot water than they had ever known existed.

Bruno had to admit that he was having fun, of course, but the results were disturbing. As he lay in the darkness he could still hear Mr. Sturgeon's voice: "There will be no more ants, no more skunks — and no more privileges, Walton." Bruno grinned in the darkness. He was accustomed to making his own privileges.

It was well after midnight when Elmer finally fell asleep. About time, thought Bruno as he opened the window and crawled out onto the deserted campus. Staying in the shadows cast by the dark building, he made his way to Dormitory 1 and tapped lightly on Boots' window. Several minutes passed without an answer. Bruno's second tap echoed loudly in the stillness of the night. Finally Boots peered out and beckoned. Bruno hoisted himself up and through the window.

"George is in the infirmary suffering from exhaustion," Boots explained. "It seems he doesn't run thirteen times around the campus every day."

Bruno just kept staring at the room. "Wow! What a set-up! Look at those stereo speakers, and the amazing TV . . . How many channels do you get on that thing?"

"Just wait until you see the bathroom," Boots said, motioning Bruno inside. "No drugstore in the country is this well equipped."

Bruno whistled. "And I thought you were exaggerating when you told me about all this! I still say Elmer takes the cake, but George sure is a strange one!" He sat down on George's bed. "Now, what's been happening? You first."

Grinning despite his problems, Boots related the story of George's mint stamps, then went on to the epidemic of creeping caliotis. Bruno found it hard to believe that anyone would spend the day dying in bed just because of a few paint spots until Boots handed him the clipping.

"Pretty slick."

"*Very* slick," Boots agreed sarcastically. "So slick I've lost my privileges for three months! And that means I can't go to the dance at Miss Scrimmage's on Saturday."

"What makes you think they'd let us in there anyway? Remember what we did the last time?"

Boots smiled as he recalled the last dance — Miss Scrimmage's gymnasium hung with pink and silver streamers, the walls ringing with music and laughter. It was just as the buffet supper was about to be served that the bottle of scotch Bruno and Boots had poured into the punch bowl reached Miss Scrimmage's head. Suddenly she ripped the chaperone's badge off her shapeless black dress, hauled a startled Mr. Sturgeon onto the dance floor and started into her own extraordinary version of the funky chicken. At that point the young ladies lost what little restraint they had and the party quickly turned into a wild rock festival, with Miss Scrimmage being the life of the party. The next morning she could not get out of bed and seemed to be suffering from something that looked suspiciously like a hangover.

"Three months without privileges!" scoffed Bruno, jolting Boots back to the present. "Mine were suspended indefinitely! But I don't care — Diane's not going to be at the dance anyway."

"Cathy will," said Boots miserably. "By the way, speaking of Diane, what were you doing with Petunia?"

With a great smile of satisfaction Bruno related the first episode of the ants and then their second coming. "To make a long story short," he concluded, "the exterminator has had to come twice — at *my* expense. I'm now known as Bad Luck Bruno in Dormitory 2. Elmer is so scared of me he just about faints when I walk into the room."

"So where is all this getting us?" demanded Boots.

"I don't know about you," Bruno replied, "but my dorm is circulating a petition to get rid of me. If it comes to you, sign it."

"But that doesn't help me," Boots complained. "I cannot and *will not* live in this hospital/stock exchange any longer!"

Bruno shrugged and stretched out on George's bed. George probably would have collapsed had he known that his bed was absorbing another person's germs.

"We'll just have to show The Fish how awful George and Elmer really are," Boots decided.

"How can we do that?" Bruno protested. "They're only awful to us."

"Well then, we'll just have to *make* them awful," Boots insisted. "Report to the old cannon at 0100 hours Sunday with a collection of distinguishable Elmer Drimsdale possessions. I'll bring some stuff belonging to George. If we can't frame them right into the Don Jail, my name isn't Melvin P. O'Neal! As of this moment," he added, "the *P* stands for 'pushed around for the last time'!"

Chapter 8

raid!

George was carefully hanging up his tuxedo and brushing off the velvet lapels. "What a superb evening!" he remarked, knowing full well how much Boots had wanted to go to the dance. "The young ladies danced like angels, and the ballroom was a masterpiece of decor."

"It really must have been great," Boots agreed sarcastically. "After all, what could be more elegant than waltzing over the foul lines of a basketball court?"

George ignored him. "And the food — a really extravagant buffet!"

"Yes, I know," said Boots sourly. "Colonel Sanders' boys make it finger-lickin' good."

"It's a shame that you were unable to attend, Melvin,

but if you insist on acting like a barbarian — "

"Just shut up and go to sleep," Boots snapped. George changed into his pyjamas, still trying to give the impression that he had had an enchanting evening.

"You know, I'm sort of glad I didn't go," Boots murmured reflectively. "Can you imagine all the germs a guy could pick up at that kind of affair?"

George sniffed and got into bed without another word.

When his roommate was sound asleep, Boots went into operation. Fifteen minutes later the window opened and out he went — along with a monogrammed money clip, a tiny cell phone and a personalized gold pen and pencil set, all clearly the property of George Wexford-Smyth III.

* * *

Elmer had not gone to the dance either. "I don't see how everyone can go and dance with *girls*," he said with disgust. "Girls are so icky! I'm glad you didn't go, Bruno. At least one person in this school besides me has some sense."

"Yes, Elmer," Bruno sighed, ready to make his move as soon as his roommate went to sleep. He watched in dismay as Elmer set up an elaborate tripod supporting a high-powered telescope. "Aren't you going to bed?" he asked.

"On a clear night?" Elmer replied, as if Bruno had suggested the impossible. "On a clear night I can scan the whole sky."

"Why in the world would you want to do that?"

"I'm an astronomer," Elmer explained. "My world is the heavens, the universe, the vastness of intergalactic space

". . . Now if you'll excuse me, my telescope is a little out of focus."

"*You* are a little out of focus," said Bruno sourly.

"Ah," said Elmer, squinting into the eyepiece and turning two knobs on the side, "it's coming clearer. Yes, I see it — the horsehead nebula!"

"Mmm-hmm," grunted Bruno. Instead of contemplating the universe, he was concentrating on the problem of getting out through the window with Elmer so firmly established there.

Elmer was providing a running commentary. "Look! Can it be? Yes — the crab nebula! Caused by an exploding star a thousand years ago!"

"Mmm-hmm," Bruno repeated. He tiptoed through the room gathering up some of Elmer's more recognizable possessions — the skull of a rodent, a signed membership in the Toronto Horticultural Society and a corked test tube bearing the label: *Drimsdale, Test 3-A, Sept. 15.* Now how am I going to get out of here? Bruno thought. I'll never get past the house master at the main doors.

Elmer was still raving about the crab nebula and was even starting to sketch it when Bruno opened the door. "Bruno, this is fabulous! I've never seen such a clear night!" The door shut silently. In a second Bruno was knocking on the door of 205.

"Who is it?" demanded Perry Elbert.

"Me. Bruno."

"You! Go away," groaned Perry. "I refuse to open the door."

"No trouble," Bruno promised. "Honest. I just have to borrow your window."

54

Reluctantly Perry opened the door and let him in. "So long as you're just passing through," he said.

"Thanks, Perry, you're a pal. I'll be back in an hour." Bruno swung his legs over the sill and dropped down onto the grass.

At the old cannon, Boots was waiting for him. "What took you so long?" he asked indignantly.

"You won't believe this," Bruno said, "but Elmer is an astronomer. His world is *out of this world*! Tonight is a clear night, the crab nebula looks sharp — and I had to find another window. Now, where are we going?"

"Miss Scrimmage's." Boots grinned in the darkness. "Elmer Drimsdale and George Wexford-Smyth III are going to stage a shameful panty raid on the young ladies."

In no time they were across the road, over the wrought-iron fence and under Diane Grant's window. Again pebbles were thrown and the familiar blonde head leaned out.

"Go away, Bruno," grumbled the girl. "I'm already grounded for a month. Haven't you done enough?"

Bruno ignored her question. "I've got Boots with me," Bruno whispered. "Can we come up?"

"Are you crazy?" Diane exclaimed. "I'll be shot!"

But Bruno was already climbing the drainpipe to the window ledge. Diane and Cathy, her roommate, reached out and pulled him inside. Boots followed right behind him.

"If we're caught . . . " Diane threatened.

"Don't be silly," interrupted Bruno. "I never get caught. Can you cut the legs off an old pair of panty hose for us?" Then he turned to Boots. "Go ahead. It's your show."

"Get the girls together for a briefing," Boots ordered, "and tell them to bring their panties — this is a raid!"

Without a word or a question, Cathy and Diane grinned and set off to gather their friends. As each girl slipped into the room, she deposited a pair of panties in a pillowcase that Boots held out. They showed no surprise at the boys' presence. Miss Scrimmage's young ladies were always ready for some excitement.

Boots cleared his throat. "Girls, this is a panty raid. We are the raiders, *but it isn't us.* We are *really* Elmer Drimsdale and George Wexford-Smyth III. Got it?"

"You've got to be kidding!" one girl protested. "George? That pill? He wouldn't raid anything if it wasn't for money. Give me my panties back."

"Quiet! Quiet!" Cathy hissed as the girls started to scream with laughter. "Do you want old Scrimmage down here dropping her bloomers in the bag?"

"Who was the other guy?" another girl asked, shaking with laughter. "Elmer Drysdale?"

"Drimsdale," replied Bruno. "You wouldn't know him. He doesn't like girls — ants are more his type."

Boots held up his hands for order, then passed around George's and Elmer's belongings. The girls fell silent. "Now, here's what I want you to do," he explained. "Plant these things around your rooms and mess up your drawers. Then wait. When Bruno and I start yelling up and down the halls, I want to hear screaming. *Real* screaming — *bloodcurdling* screaming. I want chaos and disorder. In short, I want a riot — a full-fledged riot. Can you handle it?"

"Certainly," said Cathy. "Riots are our specialty."

"All right," Boots nodded. "Everybody to battle stations. You've got two minutes to get ready."

When the girls were gone, Bruno and Boots pulled the nylons over their heads and tiptoed into the hall. "Boy, this is going to be fun," whispered Bruno.

"*If* we get away with it," said Boots. "Okay, now!"

The two galloped up and down the hallways like wild horses, shouting in the deepest voices they could manage and banging on the walls. Right on cue, the girls began to scream. They were extremely good at it — adding howling and screeching and slamming of doors for effect.

"Boys! There are boys in the dormitory!"

"Help! They're in my room!"

"Miss Scrimmage! Miss Scrimmage! Help!"

Satisfied that the riot was progressing nicely, Bruno and Boots slipped back into Diane and Cathy's room and shinnied down the drainpipe. Just as they reached the ground Cathy had a great flash of inspiration. She raced down the hall and yanked on the fire-alarm lever. At the deafening clang of the fire bell Bruno and Boots shot over Miss Scrimmage's fence, across the road and onto their own campus. At Macdonald Hall a crowd was already beginning to gather.

Boots grabbed Bruno from behind. "The stocking, you idiot! You're still wearing the stocking!" He snatched it from Bruno's head. "Now's our chance to head for our own dorms and get back into our rooms unnoticed."

Bruno nodded. "Give me some panties first. If Elmer's going to get blamed for all this, he might as well have something to show for it."

The two separated. Boots slipped in with the boys from

Dormitory 1 and tried to look sleepy in spite of the fact that he was fully dressed. "Hey, where's everybody going?" he demanded.

"Are you deaf?" someone replied. "Miss Scrimmage's is on fire!"

The boys from Dormitory 2 were also outside milling around in confusion. Bruno suddenly found himself standing beside Perry Elbert, who stared at him accusingly.

"You promised," Perry wailed. "You said no trouble. You lied!"

"No way," Bruno answered. "I didn't pull that fire alarm." Then he turned to the noisy crowd and bellowed, "Miss Scrimmage and the girls are in danger! Who can save them?"

"We can!" roared the crowd.

"Follow me, men!" Bruno screamed in delight. "On to Scrimmage's to save the girls!"

With Bruno bellowing at the head of his army, the brave men of Macdonald Hall poured across the road and stormed Miss Scrimmage's campus. Their cries of "Don't worry, girls!" and "Hang in there, girls!" were met by Cathy's ear-splitting scream, "The boys are here! We're saved!"

Suddenly Miss Scrimmage appeared on the front balcony of the residence, wrapped in a bathrobe, her hair in pincurls, her glasses askew on her nose. She was waving a shotgun and shouting hysterically. "Where's the lion?" she screeched. "Hang on, girls, I'll save you!"

BOOM! The shotgun went off by mistake, blasting a large hole in the sign over the main gate. All screaming stopped abruptly. The girls, who had been carried across the highway to safety by the courageous Macdonald Hall army, began to straggle back.

Finally Mr. Sturgeon and several members of his staff arrived on the scene. They entered the residence and investigated until they could assure Miss Scrimmage that there was no fire — and no lion. A few minutes later Mr. Sturgeon came out onto the balcony and addressed his boys. "Return to your rooms at once," he ordered. "There is no fire. I repeat, return to your rooms at once."

* * *

When he got back to his room, Boots discovered that George had not yet returned from the scene of the commotion. Whistling cheerfully, he extracted a pair of pink panties from the pillowcase and stuffed them into the pocket of George's tan jacket. The rest of the panties he pushed under George's pillow. Then he climbed into bed and promptly fell asleep.

* * *

Bruno beat the crowd back to Dormitory 2. As he quietly opened the door to his room, Elmer's voice floated out: "Did you know, Bruno, that some of the particles that make up the rings of Saturn are as big as houses?"

"Mmm-hmm," said Bruno. Unbelievably, Elmer had never missed him, nor had he noticed the commotion on the two campuses. He had been glued to his telescope all this time — gazing and drawing and theorizing.

"Elmer, old buddy, you're one in a million," marvelled Bruno.

Elmer took this as a compliment. "Thank you, Bruno," he said.

The battlefield was deserted. A light breeze whispered through the evergreens on both campuses. In front of Miss Scrimmage's, soft moonlight illuminated tattered bushes and trampled flower beds — and a sign which read: *Miss Scrimmage's Fishing School for Young Ladies.*

Chapter 9

expelled?

At precisely 9:00 on Sunday morning a knock sounded at the door of room 201. Bruno was still in bed, but Elmer was awake and dressed, taking care of the new algae eater in his fish tank. He dried his hands and opened the door.

There stood the school messenger, one of the freshmen. "Boy, Drimsdale," he said, "are you ever in trouble!" He handed Elmer a note which ordered him to present himself at the Headmaster's office in one hour's time.

Elmer collapsed in a heap on his bed. "I knew it," he moaned. "Someone must have seen my telescope at the window last night and reported that I was up after lights-out. My telescope will probably be confiscated — I may even be punished! I've never been punished in my whole life!" In agony, he hugged his pillow — and his hand closed on a pair of silk panties. Elmer screamed so loudly that Bruno bounded out of bed in alarm.

"What are *these*?" cried Elmer, waving the panties in Bruno's face.

"If you don't know," Bruno replied, "then I can't help you. I can only assure you that they're *not* mine."

"But where did they come from?" Elmer shrieked. "How did they get here?"

Bruno pretended to think about it for a moment. Then he stared at his roommate in horror. "Elmer! You?"

"What do you mean, me?"

"The panty raid at Miss Scrimmage's last night," said Bruno. "It was you! I wouldn't have believed it — I thought you said girls were so icky."

"What panty raid? I'm innocent!" Elmer screamed. "Am I going to get blamed for something I don't even know about?"

"Into each life some rain must fall," said Bruno philosophically. "Whatever you sow, you must reap."

* * *

The messenger had continued to Dormitory 1. Boots took the note from him and woke George. "Note for you, George. From Mr. Sturgeon's office."

George yawned sleepily. "Oh, that must be about my allowance from Papa." He accented the second syllable. "He always sends it by special messenger. I can hardly wait to see if I got the raise I asked for."

Boots smiled. "Maybe you'll get even more than you asked for," he said.

When George reached the office the door was open; so he knocked, then went right in. As he entered the room, he was surprised to see Elmer Drimsdale seated meekly on the bench. George walked towards the visitor's chair, but Mr. Sturgeon motioned to him to sit beside Elmer. George was puzzled. Mr. Sturgeon opened his top desk drawer and pulled out a plastic bag. From it he took out one rodent skull, one Toronto Horticultural Society membership card and a labelled test tube. He made a second pile with a money clip, a cell phone and a pen and pencil set, all clearly monogrammed.

"I believe these belong to you," the Headmaster said grimly.

"Y–yes sir," George stammered, now thoroughly confused. Elmer was speechless.

"These items were gathered at Miss Scrimmage's last night after a disgraceful episode during which some articles of — er — underwear were stolen." George began to sweat. "The discovery of these items," Mr. Sturgeon continued, "has led everyone to conclude that you two were the raiders. Unfortunately I have no alternative but to agree." He smiled grimly. "You were even identified by name by several of the young ladies."

George began to sweat even more. He reached for his handkerchief to wipe his forehead — and pulled out a pair of pink panties. "Yipes!" he cried.

"That will do," said Mr. Sturgeon. "I rather think that that strange substitute for a pocket handkerchief completes the case against you."

"But, sir," pleaded George, "I have no idea how that got into my pocket!"

Mr. Sturgeon's smile changed. "Then I imagine your thinking is a little slow, Wexford-Smyth. I'm quite certain that *I* know how it got there."

"I found some things like that under my pillow," Elmer gasped.

"I'm not surprised to hear that," said Mr. Sturgeon. "It seems that you two boys have been very nicely framed."

For the first time since he had received the summons Elmer felt a surge of hope. He still had very little idea of what he had been framed *for*, but so long as he wasn't going to be punished, his world looked as if it would keep on turning.

"Melvin!" George exclaimed. "It was Melvin, wasn't it, sir? And that uncouth friend of his, Bruno Walton?"

"Bruno," echoed Elmer sadly. "I've had enough of Bruno to last me a lifetime!"

"Is Walton harassing you?" asked Mr. Sturgeon.

Elmer shook his head. "Oh no, sir. It's just that he's so — unrestrained. And I'm so — I guess I seem dull to him, sir. I don't think he likes me."

"Melvin is certainly harassing me, sir," George broke in. "He should be punished, if you ask me."

"I fail to recall asking you," said Mr. Sturgeon, giving George his infamous grey look. Then he leaned back in his chair. "Boys, I would like to try an experiment. This is what I want you to do."

* * *

Elmer Drimsdale, head down and feet dragging, returned to his room and flopped down on his bed. "What's the matter, Elm?" asked Bruno, bursting with curiosity. "Aren't you going to crack the old books?"

"Books?" sobbed Elmer. "What's the point? I've been expelled!"

Bruno's normally ruddy face turned chalk-white. "*What*? They can't do this to you! You're innocent! You didn't do anything!"

"I know that," said Elmer, "but Mr. Sturgeon didn't believe me. He expelled me. My mother is going to kill me!"

"But you were scanning the skies!" Bruno howled. "The rings of Saturn, remember?"

Elmer didn't answer. He took his suitcase from the closet, opened his dresser drawers and began to pack. Bruno stalked up and down the room like a madman.

"You don't have to pretend you're upset just to make me feel better," said Elmer sadly. "I know you hate me and will be glad to be rid of me."

"What do you mean, *hate* you?" Bruno cried. "I'm crazy about you! I love your ants! I love your goldfish and your plants! I'm absolutely *wild* about your experiments! I'm a Drimsdologist! My world is the Elmer Drimsdale world!" On that note, he ran wildly out of the room.

* * *

"I have been expelled, Melvin," George announced bitterly. "I leave immediately."

"Expelled?" Boots echoed. "Leave? Why?"

"Elmer Drimsdale and I are being blamed for whatever happened at Miss Scrimmage's last night," said George. He began to pack his medicines into a large leather chest marked *Health Care*. "We've both been expelled and — " He turned around to find he was talking to an empty room.

Boots tore across the campus towards the Faculty Building. He didn't know what he was going to say to Mr. Sturgeon; he only knew he could not allow George to be expelled for something he hadn't done. He ran blindly, his mind in a turmoil. Just at the foot of the cement walk he collided heavily with another running figure.

"Bruno, we can't let it happen!"

"You too, eh?" Bruno replied. "What are we going to do?"

"What can we do?" asked Boots. "Besides confess, that is."

"Confess nothing!" countered Bruno. "If The Fish is ready to expel Elmer and George, he'll be ready to hang us! Listen — we don't have to say we did it; we just have to say that Elmer and George *didn't*. We're their room-mates, after all. What better alibi could they have?"

"He'll never believe us," Boots said dejectedly. "It was the stupidest thing we've ever done."

"Well, it was *your* idea," muttered Bruno. "C'mon."

The oak doors had never been heavier. The echoes of their footsteps on the marble floor sounded like a death march in some great tomb. The desks in the outer office had never seemed so high, nor the white walls so desolate.

The office was deserted, but Mr. Sturgeon's door was open a crack. Boots knocked lightly. "It's Melvin O'Neal, sir. Bruno and I would like to talk to you."

A muffled sound escaped from the inner office. It sounded very much like a chuckle, and the words, "Right on time." Then the Headmaster called out, "Come on in, boys."

On their way in, Bruno and Boots exchanged puzzled looks. What was going on?

Mr. Sturgeon did not speak until the two were seated uncomfortably on the hard wooden bench. Finally he said, "Why are you two boys together?"

"Uh — we aren't exactly together, sir," said Bruno. "We just ran into each other on the way over here."

"Very well. Now, what brings you here?"

"Sir," Bruno began, "you can't expel Elmer Drimsdale."

"And George," added Boots fervently. "You can't expel him either . . . sir."

"How odd," said Mr. Sturgeon. "I was under the impression that *I* was Headmaster of this institution. I believe I have the power to expel *any* student who misbehaves as grossly as the two boys you just mentioned."

"But Elmer was in his room all the time," Bruno protested. "He couldn't have been at Miss Scrimmage's."

"George too," said Boots. "He came home from the dance and never left our room until the fire alarm went off."

Mr. Sturgeon smiled icily. "So," he said, "instead of being able to complain that Drimsdale and Wexford-Smyth are unsuitable roommates, you are obliged to come here to defend them."

He knows, thought Boots miserably. He knows everything.

"Contrary to popular belief," the Headmaster went on, "I am not as stupid as some of you think. I was a boy once myself, you know, and I understand all the little tricks." His voice continued, colder than ever. "What you tried to do to your roommates was thoughtless and cruel. They are, of course, in the clear; I never for one moment believed they were guilty. It was I who suggested that they pretend to be expelled — just to see what kind of boys you two really are."

Bruno and Boots sat in stunned silence.

"Had you not come to me to prevent their expulsion, I would have immediately sent you both packing." He paused to let his words sink in. The silence was deafening. "However, the fact that you have done the right thing does not mean you will get off scot-free. Miss Scrimmage's flower beds and bushes have been badly trampled. You two will therefore report to the gardener's shed every morning at sunrise and work to repair the damage. Any new supplies which may be required will be purchased from your pocket money. This means, Walton," he added, "that you will join O'Neal for dishwashing duty, since your allowance has already been used up to pay the exterminators. You know the rates, I believe."

"Yes, sir," said Bruno.

"As for you, O'Neal, your privileges are suspended for the remainder of the year. Walton, at the rate you're going, yours just might be restored to you by the time you reach the age of forty-three. You may go."

Both boys stood up. "Yes, sir. Thank you, sir."

Mr. Sturgeon actually smiled at them. "I am glad to see that instead of complaining about your punishment you appreciate what was *not* done to you. Please go to your rooms — and separately. Good day."

Bruno and Boots left the office and headed back towards their dormitories.

Moments after the boys had left, Mr. Sturgeon's telephone buzzed. He grimaced. "*That's* right on schedule too."

He lifted the receiver to his ear. "Hello . . . Yes, Miss Scrimmage. I was just about to call you . . . I'm sending two of my boys over to repair the damage. They'll be working from sunrise every morning . . . Yes, Miss Scrimmage, we intend to cover all losses . . . Miss Scrimmage, with all due respect, I must ask you not to refer to *my boys* as hoodlums when *your girls* were responsible for the riot . . . Oh yes, they were. My boys could not possibly have achieved that result without inside help from those female barbarians of yours . . . I've told you, your flowers and bushes *will* be replaced. My boys merely thought they were rescuing your girls from a fire . . . What *about* your sign? May I remind you that it was no one from Macdonald Hall who shot a hole through it . . . Well, perhaps you should *teach* them fishing. They certainly aren't learning manners! And furthermore, Miss Scrimmage . . . Miss Scrimmage? . . . "

As Mr. Sturgeon replaced the receiver, a picture flashed through his mind: boys milling and shouting, girls running and screaming, and on the balcony, Miss Scrimmage with her shotgun. He put his head down on the desk and laughed until the green blotter was soaked with tears.

Chapter 10

breakfast at scrimmage's

At daybreak Bruno and Boots were trudging along Miss Scrimmage's driveway. In the grey dawn they could barely make out the ruined hedges and flower beds.

"If there was any justice," mumbled Bruno as he pushed the wheelbarrow, "I would be riding in this thing and *you* would be pushing, because this is all your fault."

Boots ignored him. His attention had been captured by something else. "Ah," he said with delight, "we were expected. News travels fast in this place." He pointed to the orchard.

Slung between two apple trees was a makeshift banner. *WELCOME BRUNO AND BOOTS*, it read. Under the sign stood a small folding table covered by a bed-sheet tablecloth and set with Miss Scrimmage's best china, silver and crystal. A cardboard sign on the table said *Breakfast is Served*. Milk, orange juice, fresh rolls and butter, strawberries and cold cereal awaited the boys.

"Those girls!" sighed Bruno gratefully. "They remind me of us!" It was the highest compliment he could pay.

Their spirits much improved by the welcome, Bruno and Boots feasted like royalty. They were reluctantly preparing to start work after their hearty breakfast when they heard footsteps rustling in the grass. Diane and Cathy soon appeared, leading a parade of girls in jeans and T-shirts.

"Detail, halt!" ordered Diane. The girls stopped.

Cathy walked up to Bruno and Boots. "Good morning," she greeted. "We're the Good Samaritan Committee. You just relax and leave everything to us." She turned to Diane. "All right. Let's get to work."

The boys watched in fascination. Two girls took down the banner and began to dismantle the table. The rest set to work with shovels and hoes on the garden and hedges. In an hour's time the hedge looked almost normal and the flower beds, though a little bare, were once more neat and orderly.

"Where were they," gasped Bruno, "when I was catching ants?"

"I'll bet they're good dishwashers too," added Boots. He shivered at the image of himself in the Macdonald Hall kitchen, up to his ears in soapsuds, earning his measly five dollars an hour.

Cathy, covered in earth, her arms scratched by the bushes, came over and dropped exhausted beside them.

"That's that," she puffed. "Sorry, but there are an awful lot of dead flowers that will have to be replaced. Maybe this will help." She dropped a battered paper bag into Boots' lap. "There's fourteen dollars and nine cents," she said. "We took up a collection at dinner time. It's sort of a contribution for Saturday's entertainment. Even Miss Scrimmage gave us all her change — but of course she thought she was giving it to the Red Cross."

"You are so wonderful," declared Boots, "that you defy description!"

Bruno just sat there shaking his head. "I don't know what to say!"

"You?" Cathy laughed. "*You* don't know what to say? The Mouth is silent?"

"Say thank you, Bruno," said Boots.

"I don't know if I can," Bruno grinned. "I have a feeling she's the one who pulled the fire alarm."

"Right," Cathy giggled. Then she shouted, "All right, girls! Give it to them!"

Before they could move or try to defend themselves, the boys were attacked by the work crew. The girls smeared dirt all over their clothes and their faces. "Hey!" gasped Bruno. "What's this for?"

"You wouldn't want Mr. Sturgeon to think you'd been taking it easy, would you?" Diane replied.

"We're supposed to have been gardening, not digging a tunnel," Boots protested, spitting dirt out of his mouth.

"And The Fish won't even see us," groaned Bruno.

"You've messed us up for nothing."

"And you're supposed to be so smart!" Cathy scoffed. "Make sure he does see you. Go to his office and report that the work is done. When he sees you he'll feel like a first-class heel. You two are the most pitiful sight in the world!"

A few minutes later the boys walked across the road and back to their own campus. On the way, they began to discuss their next move.

"I don't know," said Boots. "I think we'd better give up. We're never going to get rid of George and Elmer and get back together again."

"We're not giving *anything* up," Bruno said stubbornly.

"Bruno," Boots argued, "this time we came awfully close to getting expelled. Nothing is worth that."

"I have one more plan," said Bruno. "As I always say, when all else fails, be an angel."

"An angel?" Boots echoed.

"Yeah. You know — good behaviour, good grades, the whole bit. We've got two weeks until exams. If we can make a good showing, I bet we'll get put back together again as a reward."

"That's a great idea," Boots finally agreed. "It might even work. At least it won't get us into any more trouble."

"All right, then. Let's do it," Bruno decided. "I expect straight A's from you, Melvin."

"The amount of time I've spent washing dishes," grumbled Boots, "the only thing I'll be able to get an A in is home ec!"

"Straight A's," Bruno repeated. "See to it!"

The two boys walked along in the damp grass until they came to the Faculty Building. Boots tried the door. "Rats," he said. "How come it's locked?"

"Because it's only seven o'clock," Bruno replied.

"Oh. Well, so long." Boots turned to leave.

"What do you mean 'so long'? You heard Cathy: The Fish has to see us. We'll have to go to his house. I didn't get all muddied up for nothing."

"His *house*?" Boots asked in dismay.

"His house," said Bruno calmly.

Bruno and Boots walked across the campus to a small cottage with a white picket fence and climbing roses. Bruno rang the bell. The door was opened by a small dark-haired woman in a flowered dressing gown. "Good heavens!" she cried. "Whatever happened to you?"

"Good morning, Mrs. Sturgeon. Mr. Sturgeon told us to repair the damage to Miss Scrimmage's gardens," said Bruno. "We just came to report that we've finished."

"If you've finished," Mrs. Sturgeon exclaimed, "what time did you start?"

"Half past five," replied Bruno in his most pitiful voice.

"Without breakfast? Come in at once!" Mrs. Sturgeon bustled them ahead of her into the kitchen.

When Mr. Sturgeon came down for breakfast he found the boys established in *his* cosy kitchen, eating *his* porridge, with Bruno seated in *his* favourite chair. As he entered they jumped to their feet, raining mud all over the clean white floor.

"Good morning, sir," they chorused.

"Er — good morning, boys," said the Headmaster. He sent a puzzled look in the direction of his wife and got an angry glare in return.

"The coffee's not ready, dear," she said coldly. "I've been too busy with these poor boys."

Mr. Sturgeon looked at the bedraggled pair. "To what do

I owe the honour of this early morning visit?"

"We just came to report that the work at Miss Scrimmage's is completed, sir," said Bruno, "and Mrs. Sturgeon very kindly asked us in."

"All done, you say? That was awfully fast work."

"We wanted to get it finished quickly, sir," said Bruno smoothly. "We do have exams to think about."

"Yes — er — that's very wise," mumbled Mr. Sturgeon. "You will have to study hard."

"And they will need their sleep," snapped his wife.

Bruno and Boots gulped down the rest of their oatmeal, thanked their hostess with touching gratitude and said goodbye. As they crossed the campus in the direction of the dormitories, Bruno mused, "I always wondered if there was a higher authority in this place than The Fish."

"Now we know," laughed Boots. "Mrs. Fish. He must be getting heck!"

* * *

"That was a terrible thing to do to those children," Mrs. Sturgeon scolded. "It's a good thing their mothers couldn't see them this morning."

"But Mildred, those two — "

"I don't care what *they've* done," she interrupted. "Getting children out of bed at five o'clock in the morning and working them like animals without breakfast!"

"Speaking of breakfast . . . " said Mr. Sturgeon hopefully.

"I don't think you deserve any," she replied, "but you may have some toast. The boys ate all the porridge."

In spite of his annoyance and hunger, Mr. Sturgeon was beginning to feel a little guilty. "Maybe I was a little too hard on them, Mildred. I won't make them pay to replace the dead flowers. And I suppose I can take them off dish-washing duty. After all, it is exam time."

"That's better," said his wife triumphantly. "Care for a scrambled egg?"

Chapter 11

"congratulations, boys"

Perry Elbert teetered into Dormitory 2, his arms piled high with books. Just in front of his own door, his shoe got caught in a hole in the carpet. Perry hit the floor with a thud, his dozen textbooks landing in twelve consecutive aftershocks.

The door of room 201 burst open. Bruno emerged howling like a madman. "What's all the noise out here? Can't a guy study? Don't you have any consideration for other people? You can't go around making such a racket in the halls!"

Perry was shocked. "At least," he pointed out, "what *I* drop doesn't walk away and infest the dorm."

Bruno's door slammed shut. Elmer had retreated to the

school library — there was just no room for him in 201 now that Bruno had taken over. Textbooks, papers and charts were spread about on both beds, both desks and a good portion of the floor. Notes on organic chemistry were taped to the bathroom walls so that no time would be wasted. Bruno himself was red-eyed from lack of sleep. Exams were to begin the next day.

A similar situation prevailed in room 109, minus the mess. In fact, efficiency reigned supreme: George had hired a tutoring service to make sure he was properly prepared. He sat at his keyboard in a sort of trance as a team of professors in Athabaska, Alberta, fed him practice questions via the Internet. George typed in his answers and numbers on the screen indicated his percentage in each course. All but one were first-class marks. George was extremely upset because he had only attained 78% in physics. He was, however, running a 98% in health.

Boots had also fled to the library. He was more determined than ever to get good marks, because he was convinced that the best day of his life would be the day he could remove himself from the domicile of George Wexford-Smyth III.

*   *   *

As the days passed, the boys discovered something very unusual about the exams: they were easy. Bruno actually knew the answers! For the first time in his academic life he would not have to wait with bated breath for the test results. And Boots, who was generally a better student than Bruno, became confident that this was going to be the best showing he had ever made.

When Bruno and Boots were once again summoned to

the office, they were met by a smiling Mr. Sturgeon who waved them away from the bench and into comfortable visitors' chairs. He took two brown folders from a drawer.

"My congratulations, boys," he commended. "Your parents will be very proud of you — and I want you to know that I am proud of you too. I never thought I would see the day that you would both make the Honour Roll — although I have always known you to be quite capable of doing so."

The Honour Roll! The boys' faces beamed with delight. "First-class marks, sir? Really?" exclaimed Boots.

"I think my mother is going to want me examined by a doctor!" gasped Bruno.

They were rewarded by a dignified chuckle from the Headmaster. "Please feel free to open the envelopes, boys. You may have a preview of your results."

Bruno stared at his marks. There were eights instead of sixes and nines instead of sevens. His overall percentage was 86! Boots had even surpassed that with an average of 89.

"For this achievement," said Mr. Sturgeon, "you both deserve a reward."

The two exchanged a look of pure joy. Finally, after endless weeks of George and Elmer, they were going to get back together again. Bruno's plan had succeeded!

"As a reward for your excellent showing," Mr. Sturgeon continued, "I am making full restoration of your privileges." He smiled. "Even yours, Bruno."

The boys sat silently, expecting to hear more. It came.

"I can't understand why I didn't think of it sooner," the Headmaster declared triumphantly. "Putting you in residence with two such scholars as Elmer Drimsdale and George Wexford-Smyth III was an excellent idea. The results are right there in your folders."

"Y–y–yes, sir," stammered Boots. Bruno, for once in his life, was struck absolutely dumb.

"That will be all," concluded Mr. Sturgeon pleasantly. "Once again may I offer my congratulations. Macdonald Hall is very proud of you."

Bruno and Boots left the building in a hurry. Never before had their plans backfired so thoroughly.

"If all else fails, be an angel," mimicked Boots disgustedly.

"The cannon," said Bruno in a strangled voice. "Midnight."

Chapter 12

help!

"Ha, ha, ha," crowed Bruno. "And you think you're so smart! Eighty-six percent! What do you think of that, Elmer?"

"It's very good," said Elmer. "Congratulations."

"You bet it's good! What did you get?"

"Ninety-seven," replied Elmer.

"Oh."

In spite of his grades, Bruno was genuinely depressed. He had called for a midnight meeting with Boots, but what would they talk about? What plans could they make? Their only hope seemed to be to wait it out and try again next year when students were being paired off. But even that was doubtful: in Mr. Sturgeon's mind

Bruno + Boots = Trouble was an invariable equation. Life would undoubtedly go on, but it just wouldn't be much fun any more.

* * *

"Eighty-eight point five," George Wexford-Smyth III boasted.

"Hmm," Boots murmured, "that's a good average."

"*Good?*" sneered George, secure in the knowledge that his tutoring service had pulled him through. "I'd like to know what you got, Melvin!"

"As a matter of fact, I got eighty-nine percent," Boots replied. "And may I remind you that *nobody* calls me Melvin. *You* are nobody."

Although a reunion with Bruno was impossible, Boots had made up his mind that under no circumstances was he going to stay with George. Bruno was the lucky one. Elmer might be dull and creepy, but George was absolutely unbearable. He was mean and snobbish and spoiled — and Boots couldn't take it any more.

When George fell asleep, Boots made his usual exit through the window. The moon was in thin clouds and the deserted campus had an eerie look. He knew it was foolish, but as he dashed across the lawn towards the meeting place, Boots could not shake the feeling that something awful was about to happen.

He and Bruno arrived at the cannon at the same time. Without a word Boots dropped to the grass and sat with his head in his hands — the picture of hopelessness.

"Don't give up so easily," said Bruno. "I'm not out of ideas yet. How about this: we write our mothers and have them demand that we be put back together for medical reasons?"

"What medical reasons?" asked Boots with a frown.

"Well . . . emotional reasons, then," said Bruno

"No. The Fish would be sure to tell our parents what we've been doing," Boots protested. "That's all we need. I don't know about your folks, but mine would kill me!"

"Okay . . . so what say we go on a hunger strike?"

Boots had to laugh. "You wouldn't last an hour. Let's face it, Bruno. We've got to come up with something that will really work."

They lapsed into gloomy silence. In the distance a dog howled mournfully, and the moon slipped behind a small cloud, cloaking them in darkness.

"What'd you say?" asked Boots, breaking out of his reverie.

"I didn't say anything."

"Yes, you did. Somebody did."

"It was probably just that dog," muttered Bruno.

"That was no dog," Boots insisted. "Listen!" Both boys held their breath and strained to hear the sound.

"There it is again," Boots whispered.

"I heard it that time too," Bruno agreed. Suddenly he jumped to his feet. "It said 'Help.'"

"But where's it coming from?" asked Boots.

With a puzzled look Bruno jerked his thumb straight up.

"Great!" Boots sighed. "Now we've got little green men in distress."

"Either that or it's an SOS from the Goodyear blimp," added Bruno.

For an instant the moon escaped from behind the cloud to reveal an incredible sight: a huge silvery disc hovered over one of the trees. Glinting in the moonlight, a cable stretched beneath it, attached to a dark rectangle swinging in the branches.

The two raced towards the tree. Suddenly Boots stopped in mid-stride. "Wait a minute," he cried. "Why are we running *this* way? We have no idea what that thing is! Shouldn't we be going in the opposite direction?"

Bruno skidded to a halt. "Maybe you're right," he said, squinting towards the tree.

Just then the plaintive cry came again. As the boys peered into the darkness, the clouds parted one more time, flooding the scene with moonlight. The dark rectangle turned out to be a basket. Every few seconds a head appeared over the edge of it and a tired voice called for help.

"It's a basket!" gasped Bruno. "Attached to a balloon! And it's snagged in the tree!"

In no time Bruno and Boots were shinnying up the tree like monkeys. But despite their best efforts, they could not reach the basket, which was swinging back and forth like a pendulum.

"Hello in there!" shouted Bruno.

The head popped up. "Help!" it cried. "Can you get me down from here?"

"Just hold on," Bruno replied. "We'll have you out in no time." To Boots he added in a lower voice, "Don't let that thing come unsnagged till I get back." With that he slithered to the ground and tore off in the direction of the gym.

Boots was left open-mouthed in the tree, holding a branch with one hand and vainly trying to reach up to the basket with the other. Although watching the dangling object made him dizzy, he deliberately kept his eyes glued to it — at least it kept him from looking at the ground so far below.

"Who are you?" he called.

"Francisco," replied a voice in an accent that Boots could not place. "Please get me down!"

"Don't worry about a thing," gulped Boots. "Bruno's gone for help."

At that moment Bruno was squeezing through the window of the locked gym. He hurried to the equipment room and grabbed a volleyball net, then started back to the tree. "Boots?" he called, peering up into the dark branches. "Are you there?"

"Where else?" a shaky voice replied. "Will you get up here!"

Bruno clambered up with the net and soon joined Boots on the dangerously creaking branch. "I'm going to throw you a net," he called to the boy. "Tie it up somewhere and you can use it as a rope ladder to climb down to us. Okay?"

"Okay . . . I'm ready," called the boy.

Bruno held one end of the net and heaved the rest up towards the basket. After a couple of tries the boy caught it and tied it to the cable. "What shall I do now?" he called.

"Start climbing down to us. Easy does it. Nice and slow."

Bruno and Boots kept the net taut and watched anxiously as the boy, who was smaller than either of them, crawled over the edge of the basket and started to climb down. Soon all three were standing on the same creaking branch. "Let's get down out of here!" Boots entreated.

They let go of the net and helped Francisco climb to the ground. Just as Bruno dropped to the grass, a sudden gust of wind tore the balloon from the tree and sent it bobbing off into the night, the volleyball net trailing crazily behind.

"Oh no!" groaned Bruno. "That's the third net I've lost this year! Coach Flynn will kill me!"

"I shall gladly pay for another," said the boy earnestly. "Without you and your net, I would still be up there."

"This is Francisco," said Boots to Bruno.

"Hi," said Bruno. "Where the heck did you come from?"

Puzzled, Francisco pointed straight up.

"No, I mean originally. Where did the balloon come from?"

"Ottawa," the boy replied. "I live there. My father opened a fair this morning," he explained, "and they had that balloon for people to go up in. I thought it would be fun. But when it was my turn for a ride, the winch broke and the balloon went sailing away — and took me with it!"

"Wow!" said Boots. "Fantastic!"

"No, it was not," mourned Francisco. "It was horrible! It was very windy and soon I was lost in the fog and clouds. No one could see me." He looked pathetically at the two boys. "I thought I would never get down," he added. "And I am very hungry."

"We'd better take him to The Fish and get some food into him," said Bruno.

"We can't go to The Fish's house again," Boots protested.

"We have no choice," Bruno pointed out. "Come on, Francisco. We're going to take you to The Fish."

"Pardon me?"

"Our Headmaster," Bruno explained. "This is a school."

The three boys sprinted across the campus towards the Headmaster's cottage. "I don't know, Bruno," Boots whispered as they neared it. "The house is dark. We'll have to wake him up. He'll go bananas if he finds us roaming around together in the dead of night!"

"Don't be an idiot!" Bruno snapped. "This kid took off in a runaway balloon hours ago and hasn't been seen since. Half the country must be looking for him. Besides, if we wait until morning he could starve to death!" He reached out and rang the bell three times.

They waited. Bruno rang again. Finally the door opened to reveal a bewildered looking Mr. Sturgeon in a red silk bathrobe.

"We have to see you, sir. It's an emergency," Bruno blurted, inviting himself in. Boots and Francisco followed.

Mr. Sturgeon stood dumbfounded. After a moment he led them into the kitchen where he checked the clock. "If this is some sort of prank," he said angrily, "I do not find it amusing. Lights-out was long ago, and here you two are ringing my doorbell — together! — looking like a pair of ruffians and dragging along an accomplice. There had better be a good explanation for all this."

Bruno and Boots both started babbling at the same time. All Mr. Sturgeon could make out was "balloon . . . rescue . . . tree . . . volleyball net . . . Francisco . . . " But, incredibly, he seemed to understand. "Francisco," he repeated. "Are you Francisco Diaz?"

"Yes, sir," said the boy. "And you are The Fish?"

There was an awful silence. Mr. Sturgeon smiled thinly.

"Yes," he replied, "I imagine I am." He glared at Bruno and Boots, then turned back to Francisco. "The report of the runaway balloon has been on the news all day. Do you mean to tell me that it landed *here*? At Macdonald Hall?"

"No, sir. It did not land at all," said Francisco. "It got caught in a tree and I could not get down. I kept calling for help and these boys heard. They got a net and helped me to climb down. They are very great heroes."

At that point Mrs. Sturgeon came tip-toeing down the stairs. "What is it, dear?"

"It's Francisco Diaz, the ambassador's son who was lost in a balloon this morning," said Mr. Sturgeon excitedly. He saw his wife gaze questioningly at Bruno and Boots. "These two nice boys of yours seem to have rescued him," he added.

"Goodness!" exclaimed Mrs. Sturgeon. "You'd better call the police at once to let them know he's safe." Mr. Sturgeon went off to the telephone. "Now," she continued, "let's have some cookies and milk and you can tell me all about it."

After munching several cookies and gulping down his milk, Francisco launched into an account of his great adventure. Mr. Sturgeon returned and listened as intently as the rest.

"Oh, you poor child," Mrs. Sturgeon said at the end of Francisco's story. "Here, have some more milk."

Just then the telephone rang. "That will probably be your father," said Mr. Sturgeon as he went to answer it. He spoke briefly, then called Francisco to the phone. The boy took it and began to speak rapidly in a foreign language.

Boots raised one eyebrow. "Spanish? Or Portuguese?"

Bruno shrugged. "It's all Greek to me. Boy, if his father really is an ambassador or something in Ottawa, maybe we'll get a reward."

"Maybe we won't get expelled," Boots countered. "That would be reward enough for me."

Francisco returned from the telephone. "My father is very grateful to you . . . and very worried about me," he said. "He asks if you will be kind enough to put me up for the night. He and his staff will be here in the morning. He would like to talk with you again."

"Of course," said Mr. Sturgeon, returning to the phone.

While Mrs. Sturgeon fussed over Francisco, Bruno and Boots finished off the remaining cookies. A few minutes later Mr. Sturgeon reappeared and motioned the boys towards the door. "We will discuss your nocturnal escapades tomorrow," he said quietly.

Suddenly there was a tremendous crash on the front porch, followed by hysterical yelling and heavy pounding on the door. The Headmaster looked accusingly at Bruno and Boots. "What *else* have you done tonight?" he groaned as he opened the front door.

In flopped Elmer Drimsdale, clad only in pyjamas. He was clutching his telescope and tripod and screaming at the top of his voice. "Aliens! A UFO! *It landed right here!* I saw it through my telescope!"

Boots grunted as Bruno elbowed him in the ribs. Elmer Drimsdale in action was high comedy. Mr. Sturgeon took a deep breath and tried to speak.

"The way I see it," Elmer babbled on, "they probably have contacts here and this is a prearranged landing site." Then his eyes fell on Bruno and Boots. "Aha! You!"

"Yup," Bruno confessed. "We were the ones who met it — and there's the spaceman." He pointed towards Francisco, who was standing on the stairs with Mrs. Sturgeon.

Elmer stared at Francisco. "Amazing! He looks so human!" He approached the boy. "What did you do with your spacecraft?" he demanded. "I went to the landing site and couldn't find a trace of it."

"Who is this person?" asked Francisco nervously.

"The ship's gone," said Boots mournfully. "It vanished into outer space — and took our volleyball net with it."

"This is no time for jokes," Elmer sputtered. "There's a UFO around here somewhere. We've got to find it!"

"Elmer . . . " Mr. Sturgeon broke in.

But Elmer raved on. "Do you realize what this means to science?" he shrieked. "I could get a Nobel Prize!"

"Drimsdale!" Mr. Sturgeon exploded. "Listen to me!" But before he could get his hands on the excited boy, Elmer had darted out the door in search of the UFO and ever-lasting fame.

Chapter 13

scrimmage's to the rescue!

"We've got to stop him before he starts a panic!" cried Mr. Sturgeon. "Quick, boys, after him!"

Without bothering to reply, the boys took off — with the Headmaster right behind them.

"Where do you suppose he'll go?" Boots puffed.

"Let's check the tree," Bruno replied. They changed direction and ran towards the cannon, while Mr. Sturgeon pounded past them.

Meanwhile Elmer was steaming along towards Dormitory 2. "Aliens!" he screamed. "Visitors from another planet!"

Lights flicked on in various windows. Pyjama-clad figures, chattering wildly, began to pour out of the dormitories.

"What's going on?"

"Invaders from outer space!"

"They're coming to get us!"

"Who?"

"We've had it! We're doomed!"

"They've got Elmer Drimsdale!"

"They can have him!"

Inside, Elmer was frantically grabbing scientific equipment to study the alien craft. He ran outside and was momentarily astonished to find a huge crowd of boys milling around in wild confusion. "What's going on?" he asked.

"Earth is being invaded!" someone replied. "Aliens!"

"I knew it! I knew it!" Elmer exclaimed. "I wasn't wrong!" He ran off, still yelling, into the night.

By this time, Bruno and Boots had made a thorough search of the thicket behind the cannon. Elmer was nowhere to be found. "You're his roommate," said Boots. "What would he do now?"

"Let's see if he went back to the dorm."

They ran across the campus and rounded the corner of the Faculty Building. All three dormitories were ablaze with lights and the entire student body was engaged in a full-scale panic.

"What the heck . . . !" exclaimed Boots.

Bruno grabbed the nearest boy to him. "What's going on?" he demanded.

Perry Elbert glared accusingly at him. "As if you didn't know!"

"Aliens!"

"UFOs!"

"Invaders from outer space!" the boys shouted.

Boots tugged at Bruno's arm. "We've got to put a stop to this!" he said urgently.

"I never stopped a riot in my life," protested Bruno. "I *start* them."

"We're in enough trouble! And we've got to find — " Boots never finished his sentence.

"Who is going to defend Macdonald Hall?" Bruno shouted in a voice that carried from one end of the campus to the other. "And who will protect those innocent girls across the road?"

At that moment Miss Scrimmage's P.A. system crackled: *Calling all girls! Calling all girls! This is Planetary Defence! You are needed in Earth's darkest hour! Macdonald Hall is being invaded by aliens!*

Boots groaned in despair and hid his face in his hands. It was Cathy's voice. Then he looked up and groaned again. Pink nighties, bristling with softball bats and field-hockey sticks, were streaming across the road.

Halfway up a tree Bruno appeared, howling, "To the gym, men! Arm yourselves!"

Boots watched in mounting anxiety as suddenly Miss Scrimmage burst out onto her balcony, screaming and waving her shotgun. At almost the same moment Mr. Sturgeon, his red bathrobe flapping in the breeze, rushed onto the mad scene. "Don't!" he cried. "Miss Scrimmage! Don't!" His shout only startled her. *BOOM! BOOM!* She fired into the air.

Out of the dark sky plunged the basket which had carried Francisco Diaz — its side sporting a hole exactly matching the one in Miss Scrimmage's sign. As it plummeted to earth it struck a shadowy figure standing by the side of the road. Mr. Sturgeon ran over and heaved the basket off the victim. It was Elmer Drimsdale, out cold.

"They've landed!"

"They've killed Elmer Drimsdale!"

"Quit poking me with that stupid bat! I'm not an alien!"

"Teddy bears on your pyjamas, Howard?"

"Shut up!"

"What's going on?"

Bruno and Boots were the next to arrive at Elmer's side. Bruno dropped to his knees. "Elmer! Elmer, speak to me!" His roommate didn't move.

Suddenly Cathy came tearing across the road with a brimming fire bucket. "This will revive him!" she shouted. Unfortunately she misjudged her aim and the entire bucketful of water sloshed over Mr. Sturgeon's head! The Headmaster just sat there, dripping and sputtering.

A few drops of water sprinkled Elmer's face. His eyelids fluttered and he sat up. "Good evening, sir," he said calmly. "Is it raining?"

Just then a red minivan came tearing up the highway from the direction of the city. Its sides were blazoned with the words *UFO Society*, and the loudspeakers on the roof were blaring: *Attention, aliens. Do not be alarmed. We come in peace.*

The truck screeched to a halt beside the highway and a man leapt out shouting. "Where's Drimsdale?"

Elmer suddenly recalled his mission and jumped to his feet. "Here I am. Over here!"

"We came as quickly as we could," panted the man. "Where are the aliens?"

"*This has gone far enough!*" Mr. Sturgeon bellowed. "There are no aliens! There is no spaceship! This is all a horrible mistake . . . "

"Who's this old geezer?" asked the UFO man. "Are you trying to interfere with a scientific investigation?"

Mr. Sturgeon's face turned purple. He stood up, soaked to the skin and shivering, trying to muster what dignity he had left. "Enough of this nonsense!" he spluttered. "Students, return to your rooms at once! Immediately! I will deal with this in the morning. I repeat: there is no danger; there are no aliens."

Under the Headmaster's icy gaze, the crowd began to drift away. Mr. Sturgeon turned to the UFO investigator. "Doubtless you are able to recognize the basket of a balloon," he said. "*That* is your UFO."

"Oh," mumbled the man. "Well then, never mind." He scurried to his truck, shut off the loudspeaker and drove away.

* * *

"My word, William! Whatever happened to you? Is it raining?"

"No, Mildred, it is not raining," Mr. Sturgeon responded with admirable control. "One of the well-bred young ladies from across the road sloshed a bucket of water on me."

"Gracious! Why would she do a thing like that?"

"Oh, it was purely accidental," said Mr. Sturgeon bitterly. "She misjudged. Actually, she was bringing the water to revive Elmer Drimsdale."

"What was wrong with Elmer Drimsdale?"

Mr. Sturgeon sighed deeply. "A basket fell on him," he explained, "after Miss Scrimmage shot it down. Mildred, that woman is going to kill someone one day!"

"Yes, yes, dear," his wife soothed. "I'm sure everything will be fine in the morning. Let's not wake up Francisco. The poor child is just exhausted. Thank heaven for Bruno and Melvin!" she added.

"I wouldn't put it *quite* that way," Mr. Sturgeon replied sourly. "Those two have finally gone too far. Tonight was the last straw."

"Nonsense. All they did was save a child. They didn't create the disturbance. They went out to try and stop it."

Mr. Sturgeon opened his mouth and then closed it again. There was no use trying to explain to his wife about Bruno and Boots. Instead, he marched upstairs in search of a towel and dry pyjamas.

Chapter 14

no end to miracles!

Bruno was sleeping in. Elmer, who had not slept a wink since the incident, could only marvel at his roommate's tranquillity.

There was a knock at the door. Elmer answered it to admit the office messenger.

"Greetings, Alien Elmer," the boy pronounced. "I am the bearer of a message from Earth."

"For me?" Elmer quavered.

"Nope, for Walton. From Mission Control."

Elmer breathed a deep sigh of relief. "Bruno, wake up. There's a message for you from Mr. Sturgeon."

Bruno rolled over and yawned. "I'm too tired. He'll have to wait."

"Oh no, he won't," said the messenger. "The place is crawling with cops."

Bruno bounded out of bed and began to dress.

* * *

"I just *knew* that you and your unsavoury friend had to be behind that uproar last night," growled George. "This came for you." He handed Boots a message from the office.

"Doesn't bother me a bit," shrugged Boots with as much false confidence as he could muster. "I intend to put the blame squarely where it belongs — on you."

"You wouldn't dare!" cried George, but Boots was already out the door and gone.

He ran full tilt to the Faculty Building, where he narrowly avoided another collision: Bruno was running from the other direction.

"Are you as scared as I am?" asked Boots.

"Me? *Scared*?" lied Bruno. "Never worry about what you can't avoid, I always say." He cleared his throat. "I hear there were cops here this morning."

"Oh no!" moaned Boots. "Expelled *and* arrested."

"It's only our first offence," Bruno offered hopefully. "Maybe we'll just get bawled out."

"I hope I *do* get arrested," said Boots grimly. "I'd like to have iron bars between me and The Fish. When Cathy dumped that water on his head . . . " He shuddered — then grinned and added, "I just about cheered!"

"And when Francisco asked if he was The Fish . . . We may be in big trouble," chuckled Bruno, "but it sure was funny! And Miss Scrimmage shooting at the balloon . . . "

"And the way it conked Elmer Drimsdale!" howled Boots.

"And then that looney from the UFO Society called The Fish an old geezer!" screeched Bruno.

"And now The Fish is going to kill us!" screamed Boots.

"And the cops are after us!" moaned Bruno.

The laughter died abruptly as the boys were jolted from the hilarious past into the uncomfortable present. "Why put it off?" said Boots sadly. "We'd better get in there."

They entered the Faculty Building and found the outer office deserted.

"What do we do now?" asked Boots.

Bruno shrugged and knocked as lightly as he could on the Headmaster's door. "Maybe no one's here," he whispered.

"Come in," said a voice they recognized only too well.

Bruno and Boots walked into the office like two prisoners about to face a firing squad. Mr. Sturgeon, Francisco Diaz, and a small, dark gentleman were waiting for them.

Mr. Sturgeon spoke first. "Sir, here are Bruno Walton and Melvin O'Neal, the two boys who rescued Francisco from the balloon. Boys, this is Ambassador Diaz."

The small man walked over to Bruno and Boots. He bowed slightly, then shook hands with both of them. "I am Francisco's father," he began. "I find it difficult to express my gratitude to you. You are certainly two very brave and resourceful young men."

Boots blushed to the roots of his blond hair. Bruno's face broke into a grin.

"If it had not been for you," Mr. Diaz went on, "my son might very well have been lost: I owe you his life. In my country we bestow medals upon people who display such unselfish courage."

A strangled sound erupted from Bruno. He covered it up with a bout of severe coughing. Boots felt he had to say something — Bruno was certainly in no condition to speak. "We're very grateful, sir," he finally managed. "Thank you very much."

"I have arranged an outdoor assembly for this afternoon," said Mr. Sturgeon, staring at the ceiling. He took a deep breath and continued. "And I understand the Royal Canadian Mounted Police have some medals to present as well."

At last Bruno found his voice. "Did you — uh — mention Elmer Drimsdale, sir?" He caught Mr. Sturgeon's eye. Elmer was likely to suffer ridicule for a long time because of his UFO scare. "Elmer spotted the balloon with his telescope and started the — uh — alert," he explained to Mr. Diaz.

Mr. Sturgeon's steely grey eyes searched Bruno's earnest dark ones. The Headmaster understood. "I shall certainly mention Elmer Drimsdale," he said slowly.

"By all means! There will be a medal for him too," said Mr. Diaz. "I wish we could have an official ceremony, but I left Ottawa in such a hurry that I neglected to bring our flag."

"That is unfortunate," said Mr. Sturgeon. "I am afraid Macdonald Hall does not possess a Portuguese flag."

"Excuse me?" said the ambassador questioningly. "We are not Portuguese."

"Oh . . . " said Mr. Sturgeon in embarrassment. "When I heard Francisco speaking Portuguese, I naturally assumed — that is — er — what *is* your country, sir?"

The ambassador drew himself up to his full height and

announced proudly, "I have the honour to represent the government of Malbonia."

Twin gasps from Bruno and Boots punctuated the sudden silence. Mr. Sturgeon cleared his throat carefully. "In that case, Mr. Diaz, I am pleased to be able to tell you that, by a fortunate coincidence, I just happen to have the flag of Malbonia right here in my safe."

"But this is splendid!" exclaimed the ambassador. "Until two o'clock, then."

* * *

Mr. and Mrs. Sturgeon entertained the ambassador and Francisco at lunch. While the adults were finishing their coffee in the living room, Francisco glanced over the morning's *Globe and Mail*. The politely hushed conversation was suddenly interrupted by a peal of laughter from the boy.

"What is it, Francisco?" asked Mr. Diaz.

Francisco could hardly speak. "Read this, sir," he said, handing the paper to Mr. Sturgeon.

The Headmaster adjusted his glasses and read the article aloud: "*BANK ROBBERS SNAGGED BY NET. Buffalo, New York. Three armed bank robbers were apprehended by a volleyball net which fell on them as they were being chased by police early this morning. Almost $1 million was recovered. Police are still baffled about the origin of the net which, according to the report, dropped suddenly from the sky, entangling the fugitives. The net bears a tag reading Macdonald Hall.*"

Mr. Sturgeon looked up from the newspaper and met his wife's eyes. "It would appear, Mildred," he sighed, "that there is no end to these miracles."

* * *

Under the bright Ontario sunshine and the briskly fluttering flag of Malbonia, Bruno Walton, Boots O'Neal and Elmer Drimsdale were solemnly decorated with that country's medal of civic heroism. The entire faculty and student body of Macdonald Hall were present, as well as the girls from Miss Scrimmage's Finishing School for Young Ladies, who cheered lustily. Standing on the platform were representatives of the Royal Canadian Mounted Police, the Ontario Provincial Police and the Macdonald Hall Board of Directors. In addition to the Malbonian medal, each boy received the RCMP Bravery Medal and the OPP Youth Award.

Bruno looked down at his chest. Three medals gleamed on the front of his best navy blue blazer. He glanced at Elmer standing beside him, then past Elmer at Boots. Even in their moment of glory, Bruno reflected, The Fish had seen to it that he and Boots were separated.

The ceremonies had just ended and the boys were making polite conversation with the officials when their attention was diverted by the arrival of yet another police car. It proceeded up the driveway and halted next to the platform.

Boots poked Bruno. "New York State Police?" he whispered questioningly.

Bruno shrugged. "Who knows?" They stared as two tan-uniformed State Troopers got out of the car, opened the trunk and took out a volleyball net.

"I expect you're wondering about that," said Mr. Sturgeon's voice behind them. "It was in the morning paper. It seems the net found its way to Buffalo just in time to capture three bank robbers."

102

Bruno spun around to face the Headmaster. "You're kidding!" he exclaimed.

Mr. Sturgeon shook his head. "I *never* kid."

Coach Flynn hurried forward to retrieve his volleyball net. "I don't know how it got to Buffalo," said one of the officers, "but it sure came in handy. Thanks a lot." The two officers got back into their patrol car and drove off.

As the crowd began to disperse, Mr. Snow, chairman of the Board of Directors, turned to Mr. Sturgeon. "William," he said, "everyone has rewarded these fine boys except Macdonald Hall."

"Quite right, Jim." The Headmaster turned to his students. "Elmer, what can the school do for you?" Elmer was in a daze: he had no idea why he had been awarded the three medals which now hung on his jacket. He was merely grateful that no one was about to expel him.

"Ask for a new telescope, Elm," suggested Bruno in a stage whisper. "Yours got all banged up in the — uh — excitement."

"What's that? A telescope?" repeated Mr. Snow. "Granted. I will personally take you shopping for it next week. And what about our other two fine young heroes?"

"Well," said Bruno, trying to word his request with great care. "We're pretty good friends, sir, Melvin and I. We'd like to room together."

Mr. Snow smiled broadly. "That's certainly not an unreasonable request," he said. "William, is there any reason why these two boys can't be roommates?"

Mr. Sturgeon sighed, then spoke slowly. "Not a reason in the world, Jim. I believe room 306 is vacant. They can move into it immediately."

* * *

Boots crammed the last of his possessions into his suitcase. "Well, that's that," he said.

"Goodbye, Melvin," sneered George. "I hope you haven't forgotten anything."

"Goodbye, George," said Boots. "Uh — about all those mean things I did to you . . . "

"Yes," said George expectantly.

"If I had half the chance," Boots grinned wickedly, "I'd do them all again. And I hope Magneco goes down fifty points!"

"The next time a balloon gets lost, I hope you're aboard," snapped George.

"And I'll do my best," promised Boots, "to land on you." Then he was gone.

* * *

Bruno's departure was slightly warmer. "About all those rotten stunts, Elm," he said, "it was nothing against you, really. I'm sorry if I've made your life miserable."

"On the contrary," said Elmer sadly, "I think I'm going to miss you. Here, I have a little gift for you." Elmer held out a small glass bowl which contained a lively baby goldfish. "His name is Bruno," he said shyly. "He hatched in the bathtub yesterday. I'd like you to have him."

"Wow!" said Bruno, and quickly helped himself to some of the aquarium supplies on the table.

"So you *do* like him?" Elmer asked.

"Like him! I'm crazy about him!" Bruno replied. "You're a good friend, Elmer."

"You're a good friend too," Elmer said. "It was you, wasn't it, who got me all those medals and a new telescope?"

104

Bruno shrugged. "Well, look at it this way: since you spotted the balloon, Francisco would have been saved anyway. You're a hero too, Elm."

With his suitcase in one hand and the fish bowl in the other, Bruno left Dormitory 2. He moved slowly, almost reluctantly, until he caught sight of his old room. The blinds were up and he could see Boots hanging up the old movie posters.

"Home, sweet home," he sighed.

*Be sure to read the next
hilarious Macdonald Hall
adventure:*

go jump in the pool

the big fizzle

"Come on, Boots! Swim!" shouted Bruno Walton. His usually overpowering voice was drowned out by the competing roars of the Macdonald Hall rooting section and their York Academy rivals on the other side of the pool.

In lane number 3, Boots O'Neal, Macdonald Hall's star swimmer, churned his arms in a steady powerful crawl. His pace was good, but not good enough. Dimly he could see at least two figures ahead of him.

As he bobbed up and down at the end of the race, the loudspeaker blared: *First place, York Academy. Second, York Academy. Third, York Academy. Fourth, fifth, and sixth, Macdonald Hall. The winners of the meet, victorious in all events, York Academy!*

Wild cheering erupted from the host benches, accompanied by good-natured, though half-hearted, applause from the boys of Macdonald Hall.

As Boots heaved himself out of the pool, Bruno threw him a towel. "Nice try."

Boots nodded breathlessly. "Those turkeys can swim!" he panted.

"Why not?" Bruno shrugged indifferently. "They have their own pool. Our team gets an hour a week at the Y."

Boots shook his head dejectedly. "It really gets to you," he said. "Only two weeks at school and already they're one up on us. I sure wish we had a pool."

Silence fell as the boys from both schools watched Mr. Hartley, Headmaster of York Academy, and Mr. Sturgeon, Headmaster of Macdonald Hall, present a large gleaming trophy to the smirking captain of the winning team. Boots and the rest of his team lined up for the traditional hand-shake, but led by their captain, the winners disdainfully turned their backs and walked out. Their jubilant supporters followed.

"Boy!" exclaimed Sidney Rampulsky, withdrawing his outstretched hand to flip the wet hair back from his forehead. "I never saw anything like that before!"

"Gracious winners, aren't they?" someone commented.

"Jerks!"

"Such class!"

"They've been swimming too long! They must have water on the brain!"

"Turkeys!" snarled Bruno. "Someone's going to have to teach them some manners!"

"I don't mind losing," said Pete Anderson mildly, "but that was pretty rotten. I'd like to fix them for that."

There were murmurs of agreement throughout the Macdonald Hall crowd.

"Fortunately," announced Bruno with a diabolical grin, "I happen to have the very thing. Wilbur, you're strong. Go get the crate I hid under the back seat on our bus. The one marked *Fizz-All Upset Stomach Remedy*."

Boots stared at him in horror. "Fizz-All! I thought you were kidding! Did you really bring that stuff?"

"Of course," replied Bruno. "I believe in being prepared for any emergency. We'll mix them a cocktail they'll never forget!"

As the bus pulled out of the parking lot a half-hour later, twenty pounds of Fizz-All crystals were turning the York Academy pool into a white, boiling torrent. There was great jubilation on the bus, and much song and laughter.

Mr. Sturgeon turned to his athletic director, Alex Flynn. "I'm very proud of our boys," he said. "They suffered an honourable defeat and were treated rudely, but they're not letting it upset them."

As the bus turned off Highway 48 onto the tree-lined driveway of Macdonald Hall, students swarmed out to meet it. Across the road, a delegation of girls from the famous Miss Scrimmage's Finishing School for Young Ladies waved and shrieked to welcome the boys' swim team home. The travellers rattled off the bus in great good humour.

"Well?" asked Mark Davies, editor of the school newspaper. "How did we make out this time?"

"Oh," laughed Bruno airily, "it was a fizzle."

* * *

"My boys did *what*?" Mr. Sturgeon exclaimed into the telephone.

The call had been waiting for him when he entered his office. "Mr. Hartley of York Academy, sir," his secretary had told him. "He seems very upset."

"Surely, Hartley, you don't believe that . . . An empty crate of Fizz-All? How peculiar. What did it do to the water? . . . That bad, was it? . . . Now see here, Hartley, my boys went straight to the locker room after that disgusting snub, and straight to the bus after that . . . No, I do *not* think the crate got up and walked. I simply cannot understand how you can accuse my boys of sabotaging your pool. There is absolutely no proof . . . Is that right? Well, why don't you try drinking some of your pool water. Perhaps it will settle your stomach!"

Angrily he slammed down the receiver and sat for a moment to compose himself. An odd smile crept over his thin face, and he buzzed his secretary on the intercom. "Mrs. Davis, please send for Bruno Walton and Melvin O'Neal immediately."

* * *

In room 306 of Dormitory 3, Bruno Walton and Boots O'Neal lazed at their desks, picking at their homework. "So you came in fourth," Bruno was saying. "So what?"

"It's not that," Boots muttered miserably.

"You're afraid we'll get into trouble for fizzing up their stupid pool?"

"No, that's not it either," protested Boots.

"Then what is it? You've been sulking ever since we got back to the Hall."

"It's nothing — maybe."

"Will you spit it out?" Bruno demanded.

"Well, you know my dad," began Boots slowly. "He's a

super athlete. He was even an Olympic swimmer once. Well, he thinks the athletic program at Macdonald Hall isn't good enough. Lately he's been thinking about sending me to York Academy."

Bruno emitted a startled howl of protest. "*What*? But — but you can't! You'd be a turkey! A York turkey! You just can't!"

"I may have to," said Boots, "if that's what my folks decide. They know the Hall is the best academic school, but they say there's more to a guy's education than just books."

"But — but you'd play against me on the hockey team!" protested Bruno. "And you'd have to live over there! My new roommate would probably snore!"

"Well, maybe it won't happen," Boots offered hopefully.

"You can bet your track shorts it won't happen," Bruno snapped, "because we're going to get a pool for Macdonald Hall!"

"We?" shrieked Boots. "As in you and me?"

"And a lot of other guys."

"How? The Fish said the budget — "

"Don't bother me with details. We're getting a pool and that's that."

They were interrupted by a knock at the door. Boots opened it and took a note from the office messenger. It read: *Bruno Walton and Melvin O'Neal are to present themselves at Mr. Sturgeon's office immediately.*

"That didn't take long," Boots commented glumly.

Bruno nodded. "The turkeys must be up to their ears in foam by now. I wonder how The Fish knew it was us."

"Lucky guess?" Boots grinned, but his expression held

a certain dread. "I wonder how mad he is," he added as they walked down the marble corridor which led to the Headmaster's office.

Bruno smiled confidently. "Not half as mad as Mr. Heartless and his turkeys," he said. "Besides, I wanted to see The Fish anyway. There's a little matter of something lacking around here."

Boots groaned softly. "Bruno, while he's bawling us out is no time to start asking for favours."

"Just leave everything to me," Bruno assured him.

Mrs. Davis, smiling sympathetically, opened the heavy oak door lettered HEADMASTER and ushered them inside. Automatically they seated themselves on the hard wooden bench that was reserved for boys who had been called to the office under a cloud.

Mr. Sturgeon was not nicknamed "The Fish" merely because of his name. The coldness of his grey eyes was exaggerated by his steel-rimmed glasses, giving him an unblinking, fishy stare. He now turned this look upon Bruno and Boots.

"I don't suppose I need tell you what happened at York Academy immediately after we left," he said.

Bruno shifted uncomfortably. "I guess we already know, sir," he replied.

"That was extremely poor sportsmanship," the Headmaster went on. "Surely the students of Macdonald Hall know how to lose graciously."

"I guess, sir, when they refused to shake hands with our team we lost control of ourselves," Bruno admitted.

"And you just happened to have a crate of Fizz-All with you," Mr. Sturgeon remarked acidly. "No doubt all swim teams carry mass quantities of stomach remedy with them." His eyes grew even colder. "You boys took the Fizz-All for the specific purpose of damaging the York swimming pool, didn't you?"

"Oh, no, sir," protested Boots in dismay. "That is — "

"Sir," Bruno interjected earnestly, "Elmer Drimsdale calculates that in five days their pool will be as good as new. You know Elmer is never wrong."

Mr. Sturgeon coughed. "I am delighted to hear that. I should hate to have to approach your parents with a bill for the repair costs. Because this is your first offence, this year at least, your punishment will be light — one week confined to your room after dinner."

"Yes, sir," said Boots. "Thank you, sir."

"Sir," said Bruno, "may we speak with you while we're on the subject of pools?"

"Very well. What is it, Walton?"

"Sir, is there any chance at all that we'll get a pool?"

"I'm afraid not," replied the Headmaster, folding his hands in front of him. "We had one planned for this year, but construction costs being what they are, the budget was fifty thousand dollars short. I would like to have one because it would fill a gap in our athletic program and provide some fine recreation. However, these things can't be helped. There simply is not enough money."

"Yes, sir," chorused Bruno and Boots.

"Dismissed," said Mr. Sturgeon, waving them out.

As they were walking back to their dormitory, Boots could stand his roommate's silence no longer. "Bruno," he pleaded, "stop it! I don't like that look on your face."

"There's no look on my face," insisted Bruno, much too

softly. "I'm just thinking, that's all."

"About what?" Boots demanded suspiciously.

"About how badly we'll beat those York turkeys at the next swim meet. Which, incidentally, is going to be held at our pool — a bigger and better one than theirs."

"Our pool? The Fish just said we aren't getting one!"

"Yes," Bruno continued, unheeding. "We're not taking any more guff from those turkeys, and we're not losing you — or anybody else, for that matter — to York Academy. We're going to raise the money."

"Bruno, you're talking about fifty G's!"

"If that's what it takes, that's what we'll get," Bruno assured him. "Tomorrow morning at breakfast I want you to round up five or six guys — let's say two from each dorm. We'll meet at lunch and set ourselves up as a fund-raising committee."

"But Bruno — "

"Don't argue with me. You don't want to be a York turkey, do you?"

"I wasn't arguing," replied Boots meekly. "I just want to know who I should pick."

"Well, let's see," said Bruno thoughtfully. "We'll need Elmer Drimsdale. He's a genius. And Mark Davies. We may need the print shop. Chris Talbot would be good — we'll need some art work. And get Wilbur Hacken-schleimer in case there's anything heavy to carry. That should do it."

"What will you be doing while I'm recruiting?" asked Boots.

"Sleeping in, of course. You know I never get up for breakfast."

* * *

"Mrs. Davis," Mr. Sturgeon instructed his secretary, "please notify Mr. Hartley of York Academy that his swimming pool will be back to normal in five days' time." He smiled thinly. "Tell him I have it on the highest scientific authority."

It has been twenty-five years since the publication of Gordon Korman's first Macdonald Hall novel, written when he was only twelve. He went on to write five more books before he even finished high school.

He now has more than fifty books to his credit, including six more Macdonald Hall titles, and, most recently, *Son of the Mob* and the *Everest* trilogy. He lives with his family in Long Island, New York, where he looks forward to his second quarter-century of writing for kids.